MIRRORING LINCOLN

Books by D. Amari Jackson published by AALBC

Jelani's Key
(AALBC Books for Young Readers, August 2023)
ISBN: 9780979637438

"Dramatic, daring, and authentic, Jelani's Key is a page-turning epic chock full of culture, history, and all the things that will enlighten and inspire young readers."

—Kwame Alexander,
#1 New York Times Bestselling Author of
The Door of No Return Trilogy

The Savion Sequence
(AALBC Aspire, February 2024)
ISBN: 9780979637469

"The Savion Sequence is a masterful blend of mystery and metaphysics, spirituality and social commentary, and is as enlightening as it is engaging. Comparisons between D. Amari Jackson and contemporary authors are inevitable, but he takes us beyond Octavia Butler, Dan Brown and Stephen King into a new world in the pantheon of great fiction writers."

—Anthony T. Browder,
Author & Cultural Historian

MIRRORING LINCOLN

The Cursed Existence of Paschal Beverly Randolph

D. Amari Jackson

AALBC.com
Tampa

Mirroring Lincoln:
The Cursed Existence of Paschal Beverly Randolph

Copyright © 2025 by D. Amari Jackson
Published 2025 by AALBC Aspire

This book is a work of historical fiction. Any references to real historical events, real people, or real places are used fictitiously. Other names, characters, places, and events are products of the author's imagination, and any resemblance to actual events, places, or persons, living or dead, is entirely coincidental.

All brand names and product names used in this book are trademarks, registered trademarks, or trade names of their respective holders. AALBC is not associated with any product or vendor in this book.

Hardcover ISBN: 979-8-9997784-4-4
Paperback ISBN: 978-0-9796374-8-3
e-Book ISBN: 978-0-9796374-9-0
LCCN: 2025944943

Cover design ©2025 by Justin Jackson
Inside design: Natalie Stokes-Peters
(On Point Book Design; www.onpointbookdesign.com)

AALBC.com LLC.
15310 Amberly Dr, Ste 250
Tampa, FL 33647
troy@aalbc.com
Printed in the United States of America

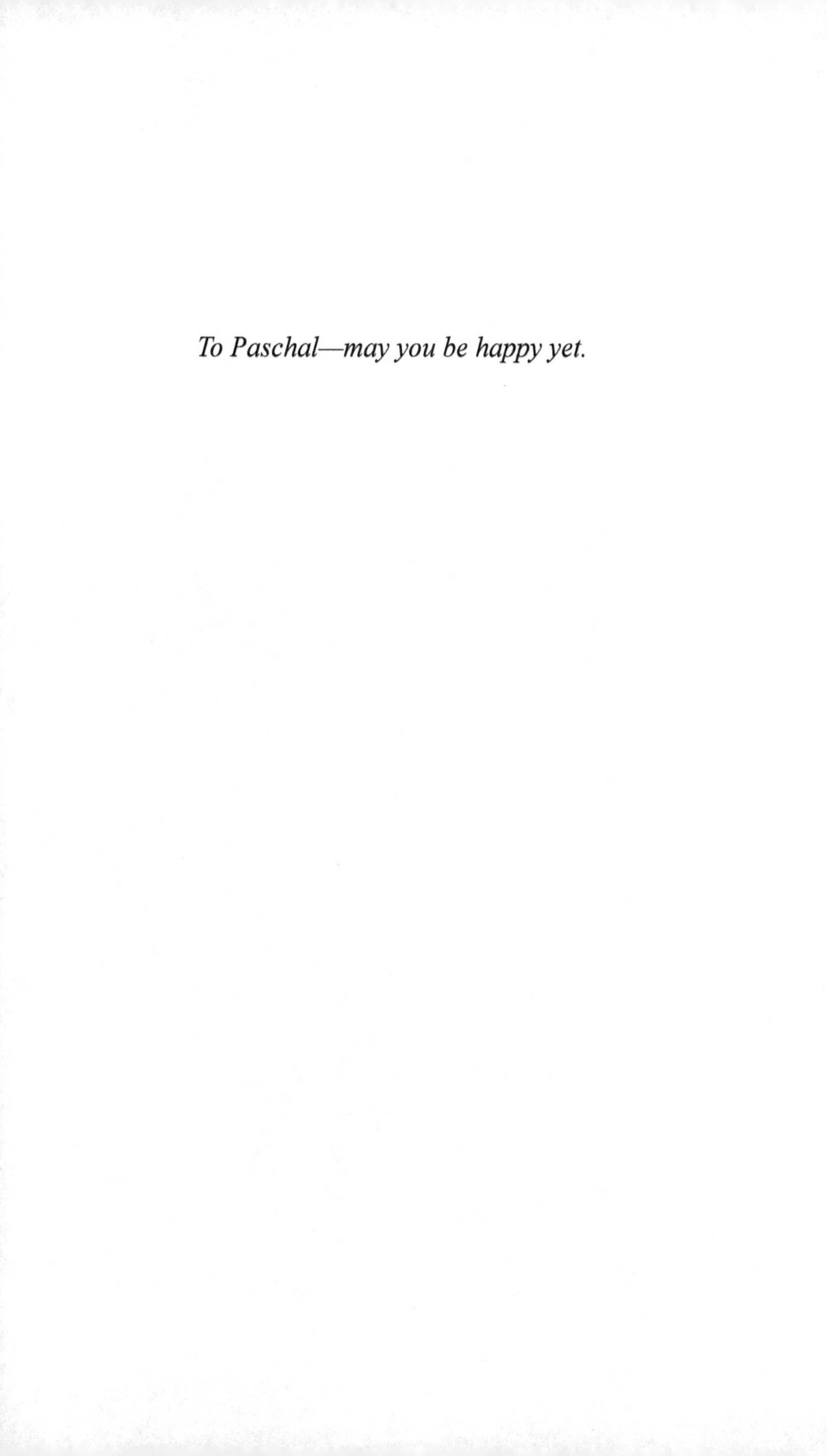

To Paschal—may you be happy yet.

PART ONE

CHAPTER I

***

THE CONFESSION

D*eath has a character, an* emblematic density where the surrounding air, formerly negligible, turns labored, forcing its grim witnesses to acknowledge its formidable presence.

The storyteller reeked of death. Bloodshot, coal-black eyes juxtaposed yellowed, cracked skin and peered purposely at the mesmerized detective. A palpable stench emanated from a tattered blanket clinging to a bony frame.

Despite the confusion of the wide-eyed investigator, two things were clear. The storyteller would not live to see sunrise. Nor would he die before his time.

For he had a story to tell.

***

"I worshiped him as much as I hated him. He was my blessing, my curse; my hero, my nemesis; my master, my slave."

The words flowed in a majestic rhythm, grandiose yet largely inconsistent with the old man's frail countenance. His eyes, still and inescapable as the surrounding room, darkened with his deliberate delivery, sucking the candlelight into his dilating pupils and somehow isolating the two men from the clocklike *clip-clop* of hooves below. His breath, labored, chilled visible, mimicked the periodic emissions of an industrial skyline. On a small chest adjacent to his carved walnut Victorian perch, a candle flickered from the draft, momentarily causing shadows to dance eerily about the storyteller's unsettling disposition.

Not quite the cold, dispassionate gaze of a madman intuited the uncomfortable middle-aged detective sitting across from his bedridden subject, Colt harnessed in a leather holster, pad in hand, writing nothing. He had seen much patrolling the bowels of the rapidly industrializing Toledo, even coming face-to-face with the rare, cold-blooded killer who could lie with a serenity devoid of the telltale eye movements and bodily twitches of the non-possessed.

But this was different, he felt, peering into eyes black as coal yet full of a special quality most returning his accusatory stare lacked.

Truth.

His silver-topped subject's words confounded this seasoned assessment.

"Fifteen years ago, on the afternoon of July 29, 1875, I was responsible for the tragic and untimely death of Master Paschal Beverly Randolph."

The detective's eyes widened from both the stunning admission in one of his long-closed cases and the bizarre referral to the dead Negro as "*Master.*"

"No, sir, the crime was not as simple as shooting oneself in the head, as you and your colleagues far too hastily concluded. That said, there was nothing simple about the deceased. He was easily the most complex man I've ever encountered."

The old man's eyes stabbed jarringly at the detective.

"But make no mistake, I am ultimately responsible for the demise of Master Randolph. And since I've anticipated this day for quite some time, I am fully prepared to confess my crime, for all its sordid details, and why I felt it necessary to facilitate the fate of a man few truly knew, a man few could ever truly know.

"Yet I did know him. And like a pyromaniac returning to the scene of a deadly blaze, I was there that fateful day in July 1875 as you and your colleagues went about your grim routine, glancing upon the bloody carcass of this strange, dark man with blank stares lacking both care and familiarity, without any consideration of who he might have been or what he had accomplished. To the contrary, your examiners were far more concerned with taking special precautions on how to handle his colored corpse given the obvious African blood that once pulsed through his slender frame. Almost as tragic as the death itself."

The storyteller hesitated, peering into the flame, revisiting the scene of death in its electric blue nucleus. The detective shifted uncomfortably as candlelight danced about the old man's motionless eyes.

"I must warn you from the outset. It is quite the story—or quite the confession, if that indeed is what it is—I am about to tell, one few would comprehend, no less believe. But whether or not you, my good sir, are prepared to believe is of no real consequence, for I have made peace with my demons and shall be judged accordingly, by an entity far more ultimate than any earthly judiciary could aspire."

The storyteller closed his eyes as the shadows seized their opening, encroaching upon the two men like frigid settlers huddling around the glowing embers of a blackened campfire.

"So listen closely, if you will, and I will tell you my story, the one fully detailing my bloody hand in the untimely demise of Paschal Beverly Randolph, a man known in life by many, but remembered in death by few. A self-made man blessed with genius while cursed by legend, a man celebrated by presidents and emperors though abused by commoners, a Seer who could gaze into other worlds yet not perceive the ill intent of those who stood before him in this one.

"I was one who stood before him. This is my confession.

I pray The Creator will have mercy upon my wretched soul."

CHAPTER II

____

THE VIEW

D_ecades before the War Between the States_, in a sprawling blue-stone structure overlooking New York's East River, a five-year-old boy had a vision.

He recognized this life was not his first, that he'd walked this Earth many times before, and knew there was a debt to pay.

He witnessed the plight of the young poet, the irrepressible romantic who celebrated beauty in all things and, if inspired, would travel to Earth's end in pursuit of passion, in search of even the most fleeting natural aesthetic, be it the prodigious voice of a youthful soprano or the magical golden-red glow of the sun receding into a still, dusky horizon.

He watched spellbound as the powerful king who ruled an ancient land with an iron hand announced a kingdom-wide contest for the much softer hand of his daughter, the love starved princess who, like the young poet, viewed romance as a soul-felt endeavor, one synonymous with life and meaning.

He cringed as the ruthless Grand Vizier convinced the king to violate his own decree and, in doing so, eternally damn the intertwined fates of those involved to an endless saga playing out through countless lifetimes, including that of the boy himself.

Years before understanding the full implications of his unique vision, the peculiar child instinctively knew this ancient drama was not unfolding harmlessly on some canvas outside himself, but rather _through_ him, in intrinsic fashion, illuminating his own role, his own soul-felt culpability. Like the sordid institution imprisoning him, the boy was cursed. And though he hated his cold, massive abode, he may as well have been hating himself, for the similarities were apparent.

Both were dark, consumed with death.

Both were haunted.

———————

Long before notorious psych wards in Trenton, Topeka, and Danvers rose to infamy, well before 63,000 deaths attributed to contagious disease and a lack of basic health standards provoked ghoulish sightings at Kentucky's notorious Waverly Hill Sanatorium, a century and a half before Dr. Harold Abramson of New York's Amityville Asylum performed CIA-mind control experiments on unwitting patients, the country's oldest continuous public hospital had already achieved a well-warranted reputation for the terror occurring behind its stony façade. While Europe had its "Bedlam"—the London-based asylum officially known as the Bethlem Royal Hospital was so horrific it spawned an English word synonymous with chaos—in antebellum America, one name conjured the sordid, near mythological image of an institution exploiting, even preying upon the maladies of its unfortunate inhabitants. *Bellevue*.

Deriving its ironic moniker from the "beautiful view" alongside New York's East River, such beauty was limited to its immediate surroundings. Despite pioneering numerous surgical procedures and such onsite innovations as an almshouse, job training center, maternity ward, asylum, and penitentiary, the Bellevue Establishment, as it was officially known, had a dark side as an unofficial dumping ground for the impoverished immigrants cramming the drooping tenements of lower Manhattan. Within its cavernous halls, treatments ranged from inadequate to experimental, from neglectful to downright gruesome. Disease ran rampant, overcrowding and abuse far too common. Botched procedures left patients maimed or dead as overworked, underpaid, and endangered providers were similarly exploited by a municipal medical establishment far more concerned with quarantining society's unwanted than restoring their health.

This was apparent in 1817 as lone house physician, Dr. Stephen Brown, had the unenviable task of caring for over 200 patients, from delivering babies to preparing and administering all prescriptions. By 1825, the hospital employed two residents to service the increasing caseload of a rapidly growing city with recurring epidemics of typhus and yellow fever. That year, both physicians became ill with typhus and one, a Dr. Belden, died, becoming the first of 27 Bellevue providers over a 50-year period to succumb to employment related illness.

If things couldn't get any worse, they did. In 1832, a worldwide cholera epidemic devastated the city and, in a ten-day span, 555 new cases were admitted to the overwhelmed institution. By summer's end, though the hospital had treated over 2,000 cases, 600 died. Five years later, amidst disease, mismanagement, and a crippling lack of food, supplies, and medicine, eight nurses undertook what became known as their infamous "escape from Bellevue," abandoning the hospital in fear for their health and sanity. They would record vivid accounts of a chaotic institution permeated by infectious disease where patients lacked bedsheets, pillowcases, and dressing for wounds, and where some had not been bathed for three months.

Beyond Bellevue, the encroaching city offered much of the same. With a population racing past 100,000, early 19th century New York was an international magnet for thousands of strange-tongued, poverty-stricken transplants crowding ships daily to take their chances in a new land promising something better than their countries of origin. For the Irish immigrant fleeing crop failure, or the young German avoiding conscription and seeking the idealized émigré experience depicted in Gottfried Duden's bestselling 1829 book, *Bericht über eine Reise nach den westlichen Staaten Nordamerika's (Report on a Journey to the Western States of North America)*, Lower Manhattan was anything but The Promised Land. Outbreaks of cholera, typhus, and yellow fever conspired with a lack of sanitation and services to claim thousands, leaving childless parents and parentless children in their wake. The waterfront teemed with plague; garbage filled the streets. Sewers were but open canals, and excrement from horses and humans mixed to give the community a palpable, unrelenting stench, one commonly noted by Penny Press journalists eager to further stigmatize a Five Points community where free Negroes settled and European women openly mixed with men of color.

Despite ulterior motives, these 19th century columnists were correct, at least, in branding Five Points a world unto itself. For the courageous Gaslight-era reader looking beyond sensationalism and actually making his way along the elbowlike Mulberry Bend toward its ill-reputed intersection with Anthony, Orange, and Cross Streets, he would have discovered a troubled, fascinating community, a landfilled cesspool where many flocked for refuge, residing in rotting wooden houses sinking into its miry foundation. He would have witnessed a place where a diversity of races, immigrants, and ethnicities—Black, Irish, German, Italian—fought, argued, and killed one another, yet conducted business, socialized, and fell in love; where gambling houses and bordellos dotted back alleys not far from houses of worship; where violent attacks on enterprising Black residents and institutions were common, yet successful Black-owned businesses with mixed patronage like Pete Williams' Mulberry Bend dance hall flourished; and where seeds were being sown for a series of infamous riots that, over time, would heighten the community's legacy of gangs to mythic proportions only rivaled by its indelible cultural impact upon the city itself.

Indeed, this was Five Points, a violent region widely unique, and at heart quintessentially American. Its streets and alleys, popularized worldwide by early visitors like Charles Dickens and Davey Crockett, would come to be known by names like "Bandit's Roost," "Den of Thieves," "Bottle Alley," and "Murderer's Row" as well as for the pickpockets, drunkards, prostitutes, and ruffians lining them. Though its key historical players had yet to make their mark, in the early 1830s, Five Points was setting the stage for the emergence of such noted figures as William Henry Lane, aka Master Juba, the free Black pioneer of tapdancing who integrated many of the venues of his day, and William Poole, aka Bill

"The Butcher," the nativist, anti-Catholic ruffian hyperbolized in Herbert Asbury's 1927 classic, *The Gangs of New York*. Like their notorious neighborhood, in many ways these two figures foreshadowed New York's contemporary racial diversity and tensions, its innovative artistic flair, its hard-nosed, territorial demeanor.

Still, for all the vice and lawlessness that was Five Points in the 1830s, the ominous Bellevue complex terrorized even its hardcore element as a place where loved ones were taken to never be seen again or, if so, less a mind or a limb. And for the traumatized five-year-old boy reared in the bowels of this uniquely checkered community and thrust into the death filled corridors of the Bellevue Establishment, nightly hauntings were almost to be expected.

Of particular concern was the recurring presence of the melancholic, pale-blue specter that hovered within his space, staring through him as if *he* were transparent, void of dimension. Before the pox had taken her, she was known as Flora, a great beauty even despite her copper hue in an era that mostly subjugated those with darker skin. Yet with her stunning facade, mixed ancestry, and royal African bloodline by way of the Madagascan throne, powerful and cosmopolitan white men strove to claim her as some sort of exotic trophy, eagerly touting her "better-than-Negroid" lineage.

William Beverly Randolph certainly fit the bill. The entitled Virginian was a member of the state's most powerful clan whose progenitors had dominated the New World by way of the Virginia colony, and the namesake of 17th century ancestors, William and Mary Isham Randolph, commonly referred to as "the Adam and Eve" of the state. A nephew of Congressman John Randolph and cousin to former president Thomas Jefferson, William's passion for the dazzling Flora burned hot, igniting a tumultuous relationship doomed perhaps less so from society's disapproving gaze than from the clash of two volatile personalities who loved as hard as they fought. The independent minded Flora was nobody's trophy, intelligent, fiery, and exacting. Their short-lived union would produce a boy as brilliant, sensitive, passionate, and troubled as they.

Flora was the only soul the boy truly loved. She had nurtured him, protected him, for all his strange abilities, and was the only one who understood, who possibly *could* understand his many life-times, his ancient wisdom, his complex five-year existence. She had helped him separate the dream world from what was real, the material world from the relentless curse that tracked him hungrily, as it had for eons.

Yet Flora was different now, her striking eyes blank, her copper skin pale, her movements slow, devoid of sound or exertion.

Cringing in the dark corridor of the Bellevue Establishment, the boy, wholly alone, ceased embracing himself just long enough to reach desperately for the woman no longer there.

CHAPTER III

***

HOUSE ON MULBERRY

Somehow *the words made sense* even when they were not supposed to. Shoe brush in hand, foot stool strapped over shoulder, the filthy ten-year-old stood mesmerized at the curb as loaded symbols adorning shops and signs sprang to life in flashes of color by way of an organic process as osmotic as inexplicable. With his deeply set eyes focused on the letters, his diminutive frame went rigid, trancelike. Time dilated and the relentless cacophony of horse-drawn carriages and soapbox sermons disappeared. All fell quiet and, alone with his vivid images, they, like him, swirled effortlessly through the aether to become impregnated by an akashic universal memory, a divine repository feeding his insatiable thirst for knowledge and containing the history of every human soul, every future possibility.

This surreal setting, somewhere between cosmos and Heaven, was the home he never had, the place he felt most at peace. Here, he could breathe, find answers, see things others could not. He could escape the grim realities of his lonely existence, hear his mother's long-lost voice. Here, he could tap into an endless source of solitude where—

"OUT-UH ME WAY YA GO-DAHM LIT-OL DAHR-KEE!!!"

The barreling carriage shocked Paschal from his trance, its screaming, red-faced driver tugging on the reins of a whinnying gelding, barely missing the fear-frozen youth. Sweating profusely, the inebriated driver straightened his path and plowed recklessly up the street leaving Paschal trembling, numb to the warm urine escaping down his thigh, saturating his loins with a circular badge of fear.

Shrieks of laughter exploded from the teenage crew of Irish bootblacks witnessing the incident from their nearby station. They had spent countless days harassing the young colored boy since they believed he did not belong, had no right taking money out of *their* pockets, a bias groomed by their parents' anger over free Negroes in Lower Manhattan pursuing employment opportunities they felt belonged to the Irish. The biggest of them, the pug-faced ruffian Cillian, pried a cobblestone brick from the pavement and launched it at the wide-eyed boy. Paschal forced his legs into motion, narrowly escaping the dense missile and scrambling wildly for minutes before stopping, hands on knees, to catch his breath and check his surroundings.

Though out of immediate danger, Paschal felt little comfort returning to the two-story wooden frame house on Mulberry. While the popular residence, home of rising actress Harriet Jennings, had its own set of hazards, at least it provided a place for Paschal to lay his weary head each night before returning to the streets he'd once slept on.

Five Points was well acquainted with the talented Brit. Recruited from the prestigious London theater scene by Park Theatre on Chatham and regularly claiming supporting roles on its world-renowned stage, Harriet was well received by men about Five Points who'd heard of her extraordinary nightly performances either by word of mouth or from her promoter-husband, Big George. Though an adept actress, many of these performances did not take place on stage. Each night, after blacking shoes or begging door-to-door to "support the household" as George put it, Paschal returned to the house of the strange couple who'd taken him off the streets and set up his bootblack box in their upstairs hallway, a few doors removed from their bedroom. There, well into the night, the weary boy shined the shoes of any man waiting on what George labeled their "special private audition with the lady of the house."

Paschal was never quite sure why Mrs. Jennings consistently made men yodel. During nightly sessions, the imposing George stood in front of their bedroom door collecting money for his wife's spirited tutorials, Flintlock dangling from a metal belt clip,

Cuban cigar angled between index finger and thumb. After counting the contributions from each aspiring actor, George would nod pleasantly to his anxious remaining guests, sit on a stool, and pull a nearby copy of the *New York Daily Advertiser*. Cued by the sharp opening of the paper, a rhythmic pounding would emanate from the room, steadily increasing in intensity, ultimately ending in what the curious ten-year-old could best describe as a hoarse yodel. The louder the yodel, the more satisfied Big George appeared, as it somehow equated to more auditions, and therefore more money flowing into his sizable hands.

Claiming to be of Sicilian descent, rumor had it the six-foot-four, honey-hued hustler was a passing darky. Either way, the point had little sticking power given the poker-faced George's valuable role as a peerless resource man who could get anyone in the local community—Black or white, immigrant or native, rich or poor, virtuous or criminal—whatever their troubled, needy, greedy or wicked hearts desired. At some point, everyone needed a Big George, even the police, who far too frequently doubled as criminals. The connected entrepreneur was known to deliver on time and often, be it guns, whores, muscle, jobs, votes, drugs, passports, winning numbers in the not-so-underground lottery, or authentic jewelry that uptown attendees of his wife's theater productions were likely still searching for. George's tan exterior was further minimized by his habit of coolly nodding and walking away from those who dared challenge his racial composition, only at some point later to quietly walk up behind an accuser, reach over the top of his head, insert his large middle and index fingers into the accuser's nostrils as if fingering a bowling ball, and pull upward while sliding his foot-long Flintlock into the racebaiter's gaping mouth. Speaking softly, the closet mulatto would then politely ask his choking captive to repeat the letters "*S -I- C -I- L- I- A - N.*"

Harriet was as striking as her smooth-skinned husband. Rosy cheeked and vibrant, the English transplant possessed a lush figure she flaunted knowingly whether on stage or prancing to a tea date at Morse's City Coffee House. She wore a consummate smirk, attractive as it was intriguing, as if harboring a powerful secret, which gave her dominion over those in her presence. Combined with her proper British accent, cosmopolitan nature, and a sense of purpose comparable to a refined madam ruling over an elite brothel, this distinct facial feature gave her an air of command despite the base method by which she supported her household.

Harriet was wholly aware of her impact upon men. They were mesmerized by her every move, whether she was dancing provocatively in a Park Theater production, pulling from her ivory-colored clay pipe on her front stoop, or attending an event on the arm of Big George. No matter how they casually interacted with, lusted after, or paid handsomely for her nightly services, Harriet's male associates, at least the less googly-eyed ones, recognized her as a different type of woman. She was one certainly not defined by the emerging Victorian mores of the day, who tempestuously led men to believe they were dominating her intellectually, sexually, or otherwise, when the opposite was true.

Paschal recognized yet another dimension of Harriet—callousness. It wasn't that she, or her husband for that matter, could necessarily be characterized as cruel since they'd have to exert some iota of emotion to qualify. She had once confronted the sleeping boy well after midnight in his closet-sized room after somehow intuiting he'd shorted the household on his daily earnings. Paschal awoke from his stained, lumpy mattress to the soft glow of candlelight illuminating Harriet's unblinking eyes, her effortless smirk. What terrified him most was he had no idea why or how long the nightgown-clad woman had been standing there.

Harriet had opened her free hand to reveal several coins which Paschal immediately recognized as ones he'd hidden in his shoe. Trembling, mouth open, his eyes reluctantly left her hand and returned to her face which, oddly, bore the same eerie expression. For what seemed an eternity, both maintained their positions, staring at each other by candlelight.

Finally, Harriet made her move. Paschal instinctively braced for the harsh blow that would surely come and cringed, throwing up his arms to cradle his head.

Nothing.

The frightened boy peeled open his eyes and saw the room go dark and the strange woman depart, closing the door without looking back. Stunned, Paschal sat in the dark, heart racing, wondering what just happened and, more importantly, what was going to happen next. His nerves kept him awake as long as they could before darkness claimed him, forcing his small, frail frame to slump downward, his fluttering lids to comfort his stinging eyes.

The next thing he remembered was something he'd never forget. Paschal awoke violently, grabbing wildly at his dark, blurry surroundings, gasping from an inability to breathe and the shock of the ice-cold wave consuming him. He was drowning. His survival instincts forced him upward to get his oversized head above water so precious air could return.

A light flooded his vicinity. Coughing, shivering uncontrollably, a drenched Paschal frantically rubbed liquid from reddened eyes and whipped his head around to make sense of his situation. He scanned desperately before settling on Harriet standing near the door, candle in hand, dripping metal pail in the other. Her demeanor was calm, as if puffing on her clay pipe on the front stoop. Her expression bore no discernible emotion.

Neither did her proper British delivery. "It would be fitting for you to maintain your current disposition until morning. You can dry off then." Harriet turned, closed the door behind her, and left the soaked ten-year-old shaking on his saturated mattress in the dark.

Paschal did not sleep a wink the rest of the night. Only fitting, given the traumatized boy who longed for his late mother had awakened to the harsh reality that his current home, regardless of how precarious, was still better than the treacherous institution and streets he'd come from.

THE LEGEND

"**D**o *you believe in curses,* my good sir?"

Caught off guard by the question and the eerie glow illuminating the storyteller's unblinking eyes, the detective quickly regrouped.

"I don't."

"Ah, of course, a *rational* man," acknowledged the storyteller, his eyes twinkling. "I wholly understand. This life is already difficult enough without adding the unseen to the opposition."

"However, Master Randolph very much did. In fact, he believed he himself was *cursed.*"

The old man reached within his tattered wrapping, retrieving a pair of steel-rimmed spectacles. He pointed the perplexed detective toward a sizable bookcase embedded in the wall adjacent to the room's lone window. "The one on the middle shelf, black binding, third from the left."

The detective complied and was stunned to discover three shelves of the case crammed with books bearing the name of the late Negro. Sensing his awe, the storyteller offered his customary spiel to the question not yet asked.

"Yes, good sir, Master Randolph penned all of those works and more. One of the most prolific writers in our nation's history, and among the first Negro novelists, he wrote and published over fifty books in less than three decades covering such topics as world history, philosophy, spirituality, mysticism, physics, botany, homeopathic medicine, and sexuality. Many of these were written when masses of his dark brethren were still in bondage."

The impressed detective nodded before locating the target and reciting its cover text. "*The Wonderful Story of Ravalette* by Paschal Beverly Randolph."

"That's it." The bespectacled storyteller nodded before receiving it, flipping it open to a predetermined page. His poetic delivery carried like music.

> *Many, very many centuries ago, there lived on the soil where in subsequent ages stood Babylon and Nineveh the first, a mighty king, whose power was great and undisputed. He was wise, well-learned and eccentric. He had a daughter lovely beyond all description. She was as learned as she was beautiful. Kings and princes sought her hand in vain; for her father had sworn to give her to no man save him who should solve a riddle which the king himself would propound, and solve it at the first trial, under penalty of decapitation on failure. The riddle was this, 'What are the three most desirable things beneath the sun, that are not the sun, yet which dwell within the sun?*

The storyteller paused to scrutinize the detective's knitted brow, inviting a response. Receiving none, he continued.

> *Thousands of the gay, the grave, the sage and ambitious who essayed the solution, and failed, left the presence to mount the horse of death. In the meantime, proclamation was made far and wide, declaring that robes of crimson, chains of gold, the first place in the kingdom and the princess should be the reward of the lucky man.*

> *One day there came to the court a very rich and royal embassy from the King of the South, seeking an alliance, and propounding new treaties; and among the suite was a young Basinge poet, who acted as interpreter to the embassy. This youth heard of the singular state of things, learned the conditions, and got the riddle by heart. For four long months did he ponder upon and study it,*

revolving in his mind all sorts of answers, but without finding any that fulfilled the three requisites.

In order to study more at his ease, the youth was in the habit of retiring to a grotto behind the palace, and there repeating to himself the riddle and all sorts of possible responses thereto. The princess, hearing of this, determined to watch him, and did so. Now, poets must sing, and this one was particularly addicted to that sort of exercise; and he made it a point to imagine all sorts of perfections as residing in the princess, and he sung his songs daily in the grotto—sung himself desperately in love with his ideal, and so inflamed the girl herself, who had managed to both see and hear him, herself unseen, that she loved him dearer than life. Here, then, were two people made wretched by a whim. Love and song are very good in their places, but, for a steady diet, are not comparable to many other things; and, as this couple fed on little else, they both pined sadly and rapidly away.

At length, one day, the youth fell asleep in the grotto, and his head rested directly over a fissure in the rock through which there issued a very fine and subtle vapor, which had the effect of throwing the young man in a trance, during which he fancied he saw the princess herself, unveiled, and more lovely than the flowers that bloomed in the king's garden. He also thought he saw an inscription, which bade him despair not, but try, and, at the same time, there flowed into his mind this sentence... 'There is no difficulty to him who truly wills.' Along with this there came a solution of the king's riddle, which he remembered when he awoke, and instantly proclaimed his readiness to attempt that which had cost so many adventurers their lives.

The storyteller checked on the mesmerized detective. "Still with me, sir?"

"Continue."

Accordingly, the grandest preparations—including a man with a drawn blade ready to make the poet shorter by the head if he failed—were made, and, at an appointed hour, all the court, the princess included, convened in the largest hall of the palace. The poet advanced to the foot of the throne, and there knelt, saying, 'O king, live for ever! What three things are more desirable than Life, Light and Love? What three are more inseparable? and what better cometh from the sun, yet is not the sun? O king! Is thy riddle answered?

True!' said the king. 'You have solved it, and my word shall be kept!' And he straightway gave commands to have the marriage celebrated in royal style...

Now, it so happened that the Grand Vizier had hoped by some means to get a solution of the riddle, and secure the great prizes for a young son of his own; and, as soon as the divan was closed, that very day, he hastened to the closet of the king, and there still further poisoned the mind of his master against the victor, by charging him with having succeeded through the aid of sorcery, which so enraged the king that he readily agreed to remove the claimant by means of a speedy, secret, and cruel death that very night...

"Such *treachery*," noted the storyteller, shaking his head at the brow-bent detective. Sighing, he continued.

The poet was drugged in his wine at the evening banquet, conveyed to a couch openly, and almost immediately thereafter removed to the chamber allotted to the refractory servants of the court. This apartment was under ground, and the youth, being thrown violently on the floor, revived, and was astonished to find himself bound hand and foot in presence of the king, his vizier, a few soldiers, and—death; for he saw at a glance that his days were numbered. He defended himself from the charge of sorcery, but in vain. He was doomed to die.

The sword fell, and, as it reached the neck of the victim, he uttered the awful words, 'I curse ye all who—' the rest of the sentence was spoken in eternity; but there came a clamor and a clangor as of a thousand protesting spectral voices, and one of them said, in tones of thunder, 'This youth, by persistence of will, had unbarred the gates between this world and that of mystery. He was the first of his... race that ever achieved so great an honor.

And ye have slain him... and he hath cursed thee...

The old man suddenly exploded into a violent coughing spell. The book freed itself from his spotted, leathery hands, sliding along his blanketed frame, past the bed, reaching the floor with a thud.

———————

Though few label it as such, nineteenth century America was the Age of Spirits, a compelling historical era our nation has largely hidden from itself, as nations often do when their current political trajectories are inconsistent with the disruptive realities of their pasts, the inconvenient and telling truths challenging the faux nationalistic identities they seek to preserve.

Indeed, these were prophetic times where presidents, like their ancient Oracle-consulting predecessors, sought answers from both spiritual leaders and metaphysical rituals, a period where lines drawn between the esoteric realm and daily life were far less distinct. The land was awash in a magical, cyclical energy as the realm of possibility had once again opened up to become more magnetic, more inclusive. Magi and mystic alike shed their shadowy cloaks and greeted the light of day with methods designed to navigate and impact the natural world about them. Spiritual counsel enjoyed high demand, séance, in vogue.

Such activity went on privately for years with the ongoing relevance of Sweden's Emanuel Swedenborg and Germany's Franz

Mesmer, mid-1840s works by New York's Andrew Jackson Davis, and the Shaker and Quaker ideologies of the day. However, the consensus start date for the Spiritualist movement was April 1, 1848 when, in Hydesville, New York, two teenagers known as the Fox sisters reported they had communicated with the ghost of a man murdered at their house prior to their family's occupancy. The reports, covered in the *New York Tribune* and then by other papers domestically and abroad, represented Spiritualism's initial public face, its alleged capacity for interacting with the deceased and the supernatural through mediumship, séance, and other phenomenal processes.

The Fox sisters' inexplicable interaction with the spirit realm through rappings and knockings became a national phenomenon as the teens demonstrated their otherworldly capacities at packed venues across the country. Their success spawned local movements in many states as séance, trance, and mediumship became the rage, particularly for those citizens looking to augment their existing religious dogma. Swedenborg had already promoted an alternative vision of Heaven, one transforming it from its traditional, static, hard-to-reach representation to an earthlier, more fluid construct where spirits interacted with humans; where the individual, rather than religious authority, was prioritized; where séance portrayed a tangible rendering of an afterlife; and where the immortality of the soul was recognized. Consistently, such ideological positioning lent itself to more progressive and socialistic notions regarding human rights, women's suffrage, and the abolition of slavery.

Spiritualism was one of the few means by which women could speak in public. An avalanche of female mediums entered the space championing a range of "spirit-endorsed" causes advancing the status of women and the expansion of citizenship. The more popular among them included young trance lecturer, Cora (Hatch) Scott, and Achsa Sprague, an abolitionist and women's rights advocate who credited the spirit realm with her recovery from life-threatening rheumatic fever. Victoria Woodhull, the 19th century leader of the women's suffrage movement and the first woman to run for president, was a vocal spiritualist who advocated for women's rights, labor reform, and "free love," the latter stressing the right of women to marry, divorce, and bear children without government interference or social restriction. For her progressive platform, and the threat it posed to the social and Christian mores of the day, Woodhull was stamped with the skewed media moniker, "Mrs. Satan."

The uncivil conflict of the 1860s served as a gruesome, effective recruitment tool for the Spiritualist cause. Their ranks swelled by the millions as a nation of survivors hoped to access thousands of loved ones lost on the blood-soaked battlefields of North and South who they never properly buried or bid farewell. The movement provided a means of coping with devastating loss, of connecting with those beloved family members and friends no longer in the physical.

A product of the spiritual era in which he lived—and despite ongoing efforts of establishment historians to negate his paranormal proclivities or attribute them to the mental challenges of his grief-stricken first lady—Abraham Lincoln's metaphysical predilections were apparent. Well before his appearance on the world stage, Lincoln expressed a belief in the prophetic capacities of dreams and visions, wrote and spoke words indicative of this belief and, once in the White House, acted consistently, be it his attendance at seances or his interaction with numerous spiritual advisors. Given the tumultuous and deadly times he endured, suffering both personal loss and the mass casualties of war, Lincoln was not much different than the millions he presided over in seeking spiritual solace.

Along with the war, ongoing developments in the realms of science, industry, and technology contributed to the expansion of 19th century spiritualism. The emergence of fossilized and geologic data depicted an Earth much older than the Bible claimed, and there were key advancements in modes of communication and transportation including messaging, telephony, and travel. Additionally, important developments in scientific philosophy and experimentation included John Dalton's atomic theory, Charles Darwin's process of natural selection, Dmitri Mendeleev's periodic table of elements, and revelatory work in electromagnetism and thermo-dynamics by the likes of Michael Faraday, Andre-Marie Ampere, and James Clerk Maxwell. These major events, at least, challenged and, at most, overturned longstanding traditions and beliefs of the day, facilitating a mass questioning of reality, the material world, and the great beyond.

Such otherworldly matters were, as the term implies, border-less. In England, the scientific and technological progress of the Victorian era was accompanied by a rapid increase in supernat-ural practices, mostly galvanized in 1852 with an impactful trip to London by American medium Maria B. Hayden. Hayden con-ducted dramatic séances, chock full of spirit messages and table rappings, subsequently emulated by a host of local mediums. However, Hayden was certainly not the first Spiritualist on British soil; six years earlier, on July 15, 1846, Georgiana Eagle demon-strated her capacity for clairvoyance before the Queen herself at Osborne House on the Isle of Wight. Queen Victoria and Prince Albert were reported to have participated in séances going back at least this far and, fifteen years later, after Albert's death from typhoid, the melancholic monarch would enlist 13-year-old Robert James Lees from Leicester along with her personal attendant, John Brown, as mediums for séances at Windsor Castle to receive mes-sages from her late husband.

In France, another 13-year-old named Angélique Cottin, a peasant girl from a tiny village in Normandy, gained attention in the early 1840s by overturning heavy tables and tossing large piec-es of furniture without touching them. Her reputation grew, and she was sent to Paris where it was concluded by the scientists of the day that Cottin was charged with some sort of electric fluid en-abling her to move large objects. She subsequently became known as "the electric girl" across France, a nation that, not long after, would be ruled by the mystically inclined emperor, Napoleon III.

Back in America, one of the most prominent Spiritualists and trance mediums of the Civil War era was a Negro by the name of Paschal Beverly Randolph. An abolitionist and staunch support-er of women's rights and sexual freedoms, Randolph's popularity grew with his mystical demonstrations, lectures in cities across the country, world travels, and his prolific authoring of popular books on scientific, medicinal, sexual, and spiritual topics, one of which had just slipped from the grasp of a dying man confessing to a startled detective in a candlelit bedroom on the second floor of a two-story structure in late 19th century Toledo.

Chest heaving from the fit of coughing, the storyteller struggled to regain his composure.

"Please forgive me, my dear sir. If I had invited you over earlier in my days, I promise I would have been far more hospitable."

The old man smiled weakly while pulling the blood-speckled handkerchief from his chest pocket to dab his mouth. He then reached toward the floor, freezing halfway before collapsing back to his former position.

Realizing the old man was attempting to retrieve the book, the detective positioned to rise but was stopped by a wave of the old man's hand.

"Don't need it, my good sir. I know the story well enough. If you don't mind, I will summarize the rest so I can ensure I'll still be around for the ending." Dabbing his mouth once more, the storyteller continued. "Let's see, the curse. Yes, that dreadful curse for such an unjust execution.

The sword fell and the victim uttered those awful words, 'I curse ye all who…' The rest of the sentence was spoken in eternity; but there came a clamor and a clangor as of a thousand protesting spectral voices, and one of them said, in tones of thunder, 'This youth, by persistence of will, had unbarred the gates between this world and that of mystery… and ye have slain him, and he hath cursed thee…'

A curse further empowered by the hasty midnight burial of the poet's remains beneath the balcony of the distraught

*princess where, every day, her endless tears would plum-
met earthward and, unbeknownst to her, water the bones
of her vanished love, nurturing them and the curse they
carried, by reason of which thou, O king! and thou, O
vizier! and the dead man, have all changed the human for
another nature, as all shall continue, down through the
ages, reincarnating from form to form, eternally damned,
in an endless saga, with the king, ever tempted by the
conniving vizier, ever thwarted by the poet, ever aspiring
to reclaim his full kingdom, power, and adoration.*

The storyteller's eyes dropped from the invisible canvas above
the detective's head portraying the vivid legend. He paused, gasped
for a breath, then spoke in plain, more direct language.

"It is said the curse grows stronger with each subsequent cycle, each time it repeats the saga. The only way the king can beat
the curse is to regain his kingdom or some lofty and equivalent
public position in his respective era—say a beloved senator or
president—despite the relentless obstacles orchestrated by the reincarnating poet, and betrayal by the reincarnating vizier."

His glimmering eyes darted back at the detective as if teasing a
powerful secret. "Quite the challenge, my good sir."

CHAPTER V

LOST AT SEA

It was time for Paschal to strike back. Weak and ineffective at his role, useless by the jaded standards of crusty seafarers, the out-of-place teen had quickly become the butt of every crewmember's joke aboard the *Phoebe*, the New Bedford-based shipping vessel covering the New England to Cuba to England circuit. Two months of cruelty on the high seas at the hands of inebriated sailors was becoming unbearable and the disillusioned cabin boy wondered if Harriet Jennings' callous neglect was as untenable as previously thought.

His crewmates had enthusiastically brutalized him as if they lived for it, as if their sole claim to happiness within their collective plight at sea depended upon it. They ridiculed the wide-eyed lad, bullying him when he served them and cleaned their filthy quarters, beating him regardless of how effectively he did so. As far as they were concerned, Paschal had been placed on the sizable vessel for their pathological pleasure and they were committed to spending their downtime from their grueling and precarious daily responsibilities making his already difficult existence more so.

Even without such pathology, work on commercial vessels in the 1840s was dangerous enough. The open sea had its share of hazards, be it the high tides or extreme weather that could smash a ship into a floating cemetery, seasoning its tumultuous waters with bodies and an array of merchandise including sugar, flour, butter, lard, pork, liquors, beans, chocolate, fish oil, snuff, cotton, nails, soap, glassware, candles, cutlery, and clothing.

The same applied to whaling. It was a lucrative industry, at least for those vessel owners and agents receiving the lion's share of revenues from such end products as sperm oil, ambergris, whalebone, and whale oil. However, for lowly paid crewmembers chasing 45-ton sperm whales about unpredictable seas, the industry was a hazardous, far less rewarding endeavor commonly ending in gruesome injury, lost lives, and lost vessels. Once a lookout, precariously perched on a mast one hundred feet above deck, located the telltale vapor plume of a whale's breath, his *"dar she blows"* signal prompted a frenzy on deck with excited crewmembers scurrying to launch the whaleboats for the hunt, racing each other to get to the whale first. Rowing frantically, facing the stern of the boat, the laboring crewmen could not see their dangerous prey given the boatheader was the only one looking forward while steering the vessel and cursing the men to go faster. Closing in, the crew would paddle softly or, if wind permitted, throw up a mast and sail and approach quietly, since whales were known for their acute hearing. Mere feet away from the massive mammal, the harpooneer would retrieve his hooked weapon, one specifically designed to penetrate blubber and secure the whale to the boat, rather than kill. Silently, the crew would await the *"give it to him"* command of the boatheader and, once issued, the harpooneer would launch his barbed weapon into the whale's endless back. All hell would break loose when the wounded prey thrashed in pain, the boatheader shouting *"Stern all! Stern all, for your lives!"* The crew would rapidly back the boat away to avoid its destruction at the massive jaws or tail of the diving, circling behemoth while allowing the smoking line—so named due to the high velocity by which this harpoon line unraveled from the loggerhead and smoked from friction—to run out and prevent the boat from being dragged down with the whale. If the line became snagged, the boat and its crew could quickly be dragged to a watery grave. If a seaman got caught in the smoking line, they could be dismembered, killed, or pulled from the boat and drowned.

Once the injured, rapidly moving mammal surfaced to breathe, the bound boat would bounce about, drenching the wide-eyed crewmen who hung on praying their boat would not be smashed or dragged so far from the ship it could not locate them. When the whale finally tired, the crew would pull the line to draw the boat close to the struggling creature while the boatheader and harpooneer risked life and limb to change places. Bearing a lance, the boatheader maneuvered forward before plunging the piercing instrument into the whale's heart or lungs, causing it to spout blood. The boat would retreat as the fascinated crew witnessed the dying colossus circle desperately in an ultimate pattern known as the *flurry* before bashing the water with its giant tail, shuddering, and turning *fin out*, over on its side.

Even with the dangers awaiting them, the reasons for Black boys and men to ship out of America's popular 19th century ports, be it New Orleans, Charleston, Mobile, Newport, Philadelphia, Baltimore, New York, or New Bedford, were substantial. Given the country's antebellum dominance in the whaling industry, and its secondary position only to Great Britain in the mercantile realm, opportunities at sea were ripe for those willing to endure its perils. Consistently, cabin boys, cooks, sailors, and ship hands on commercial and whaling vessels were among the few jobs available to Black males, enabling those who signed up to make a wage, albeit a small one, while traveling the world and, if able, educating and immersing themselves in the foreign cultures they experienced. For the formerly enslaved who'd escaped bondage and made their way to one of the nation's busy ports, these positions provided a meager means of existence superior to the hell they'd come from. Such a practice dated back to the colonial period when Revolutionary War martyr, Crispus Attucks, ran away from the Framingham, Massachusetts plantation enslaving him and spent twenty years as a merchant seaman and whaleman before famously giving up his life in the Boston Massacre of March 1770.

For Paschal, his watery hell had no end in sight. The hazing endured on the *Phoebe* had become unbearable and the teenage cabin boy was ready to make his stand. Alone in his quarters, a cabin nearly as cramped as his room at the Jennings' home, he retrieved the gallon of rum he'd hidden from his liquor-lusting crewmates and added a half ounce of croton oil, an aggressive purgative, before resealing the jug and placing it in public view where it was sure to be stolen. It didn't take long before several brutish sailors spotted the seductive porcelain jug sitting inside the cabin boy's partially open door, charged it recklessly, and took hearty swigs until none was left.

The men returned to deck where Paschal watched them closely as they roughhoused with one another, laughing wildly. Three minutes in, the laughter began to subside and, one by one, the sailors' expressions changed from gleeful to perplexed, then to nauseous, then to outright horror. Eyeballs raced wildly, complexions turned ghastly gray. Each man doubled over in pain, clutching his stomach as if birthing a reluctant baby whale. A mad dash to the nearest head ensued as the handicapped seamen battled for access, cursing the high heavens and fumbling to unfasten their britches. Once in position, chaos ruled for the better part of twenty minutes.

It was the first time anyone on the sizable vessel had ever heard the cabin boy laugh. Squealing like a stuck pig while shaking violently, tears squirting from the corners of his eyes, Paschal's eruption was only rivaled by that of his unwitting victims. The remaining sailors on deck looked on in stunned amusement, heads turning in unison from the location of the tormented seamen to that of the animated cabin boy as if observing a tennis match. One by one, recognition claimed their expressions as they pieced together what had taken place. Though unsure of all the details, this was a secondary concern. What mattered most was they had all been blindsided by the extraordinary event that had apparently transpired. The cabin boy had made his stand.

For Paschal, this was *his* moment. It belonged to him and him alone, and for the first time in years he was not the least bit preoccupied with what would come next. The anguish he saw in the sailors' watery eyes as they swore in a variety of dialects at the very gods who created them was a distorted, comedic reflection of his own pain, his own unrelenting trauma. It was as if this one bold act had somehow encapsulated a lifetime of duress—the absence of his father, the loss of his mother, his impoverished childhood, the daily discrimination and brutalities, the ever-present curse. It also served as an ultimate response to those who'd hurt him, be it the wealthy white parent who never loved him, the Irish teens who'd hounded him, the couple who'd neglected him, or the seamen who now threatened to kill him once they could pry their volatile bottoms away from the head.

Unfortunately, Paschal's big moment also masked his own growing displeasure with himself. Damned before birth, both by the ancient legend and a biblical "Curse of Ham," the struggling 17-year-old despised his own weakness, his hue, his eccentricities, his haunted visions—his own existence. As his laughter gave way to tears, Paschal recognized, once and for all, there was no place on Earth for someone like him, and if he were to suddenly disappear into the deep and endless waters below, no one would miss him. He was wholly alone in the world, a peculiar bird among hovering wolves, and those wolves were now closing in for what he sincerely hoped was the final kill.

Pissed from being literal butts of the joke, the affected sailors emerged from the head drawn, tense, dehydrated, and looking for blood. They scoured the brig and, finding the terrified cabin boy cowering in a broom closet off the chow hall, beat him mercilessly.

It was more than the already troubled teen could take. Spending the night weeping and tending to his bruises, he waited until most of the crew was asleep before taking to the starlit deck, past two unwitting deckhands—one inebriated, the other asleep—and heading toward the bow. Though the vastness of the night sea mirrored the infinity of the twinkling heavens above, the distraught teen felt broken and trapped in the middle of an ocean closing in on him, no land or friend in sight.

Paschal knew what he had to do. Tears escaping his swollen face, he closed his eyes and took off running toward the ship's bow, skirting its curved tip, and launching his battered frame into midair, high above the icy waters of the endless Atlantic.

CHAPTER VI

FORWARD BENDS HIS HEAD

"Sailors, to a man, are superstitious, though less so now than in the days whereof I am speaking. Still, at present, it is not hard, in spite of the march of intellect, to find sailors who, between the dog-watch and eight bells, will spin you a yarn under the weather rail that will make a man's hair stand on end like hairs on an enraged kitten.

On board the Phœbe there were several old salts, and many were the tales they told of the ghosts of murdered sailors, appearing in the midst of dreadful storms, to encourage foremast Jacks, and frighten the souls of guilty mates and captains; and of course all this tended to deepen the vein of superstition and mysticism running through me."

Brow bent, the detective looked on as the storyteller stopped reading Randolph's *The Wonderful Story of Ravalette*, closed his blood-shot eyes, and began an eerie recitation. The candlelight dimmed.

And now the storm-blast came, and he
Was tyrannous and strong:
He struck with his o'ertaking wings,
And chased us south along.

With sloping masts and dipping prow
As who pursued with yell and blow
Still treads the shadow of his foe,
And forward bends his head,
The ship drove fast, loud roared the blast,

The southward aye we fled.

And now there came both mist and snow,
And it grew wondrous cold:
And ice, mast-high, came floating by,
As green as emerald.

And through the drifts the snowy clifts
Did send a dismal sheen:
Nor shapes of men nor beasts we ken—
The ice was all between.

The spell was broken. The detective's eyes softened with recognition.

"Samuel Taylor Coleridge." He nodded. "*The Rime of the Ancient Mariner*. When I was a boy, my father would recite it to me whenever he took me out on the water."

"Then apparently your father was a learned and wonderful man, my good sir," said the old man, his eyes twinkling through spectacles. He repositioned *Ravellete* and resumed reading.

Often have I been apprised of the presence and power of the dead or of those who never die, and, when tempted to share the dangerous pleasures of my older comrades, been mysteriously saved.

Sailors, like everybody else, are fond of power, and delight in lording it over those whom chance or accident places in their power; and on every vessel there is one man who is sure to be the butt and target for petty tyranny and abuse. On board the Phœbe this fell to my lot...
At last I meditated suicide as a relief, and, in a paroxysm of rage and despair, such as boys only are subject to, actually ran aft to accomplish it by leaping over the taffrail into the surging sea...

I was arrested by a narrow blast of warm—almost hot air, which thrilled me to the very center of my being, and almost pinned me to the deck, while at the same time there

*flowed into my soul an eloquent and indignant protest
against my supreme folly, accompanied by the spoken
words, 'Be patient! Try!*

———————

Whether divine intervention or climactic anomaly, the wind was now at Paschal's back. Despite the beating he'd received, none of the sailors were fool enough to mess with the vengeful little cabin boy. Simultaneously, Paschal took advantage of his new lease on life, now viewing his purpose on board the ship and, by extension, his life purpose as a spiritual explorer well positioned to travel the world. For the better part of the 1840s, his menial position on the *Phoebe* and other brigs and whalers shipping out of northeastern ports afforded Paschal a free ticket to experience many of the countries, cultures, languages—and women—about the globe, as well as the time to study them in person and through associated literature.

In Cuba, he witnessed the tense environment in the aftermath of the *Año del Cuero,* the June 1844 execution and imprisonment of thousands of Afro-Cubans in Havana, both enslaved and free, for the *Conspiración de La Escalera,* a rumored revolt to rid the Spanish colony of slavery.

In India, amidst increasing tensions between an aggressive British East India Company and the Sikh Empire, he was exposed to the ancient erotic teachings of the *Kama Sutra* through intimate relations with a Delhi courtesan well-schooled in the arts of seduction and sexuality.

In Germany, Paschal studied the varied ideologies of Hegel while observing the unrest facilitated by heavy taxation and political censorship, ultimately spawning liberal reforms in many of the German states.

In England, he encountered the shaky emergence of the Victorian era, its reforms, and substantial challenges including stark rises in poverty, population, rural unemployment, and migration to English towns by starving residents from both the English and Irish countrysides escaping the destructive famine of the latter half of the decade. Like many around the world, Paschal was stunned as millions died from hunger and disease in territories governed by Britain, long regarded the most stable, progressive, and prosperous nation in the world.

On land or at sea, at home or abroad, the Massachusetts-based autodidact read incessantly, whatever books he could get his hands on, be it Dickens' *A Christmas Carol*, Dumas' *The Count of Monte Cristo*, Brontë's *Wuthering Heights*, and the short stories of Poe along with the philosophical, medical, esoteric, erotic, and scientific offerings of Plato, Euclid, Vātsyāyana, Swedenborg, Mesmer, Kant, Rousseau, Newton, Franklin, John Gunn, René Laennec, and John Dee. Between shipping gigs, Paschal bounced about the region studying and practicing mysticism, homeopathy, and the dyer's and barber's trades as an additional means of supporting himself and his rapidly growing library.

In 1848, the commonly regarded birthyear of American spiritualism, the worldly 22-year-old, inspired by a trip to Litchfield, Michigan where he observed the paranormal proclivities of two siblings, capitalized on his superior intellect, capacity for clairvoyance, and knowledge of foreign cultures to present himself as a medium. Using the antique mirror he inherited from his mother, Paschal mesmerized onlookers by communicating with his deceased matriarch and engaging spirits from other worlds, past and future. His audiences and reputation grew quickly as Spiritualists from about the Northeast flocked to experience the widely touted demonstrations of the "clairvoyant physician." Given the rapid proliferation of seances in the region, Paschal made his mark by falling into trance and channeling the full and unbroken philosophies, often in their native languages, of such popular figures as Ben Franklin, Julius Caesar, Mohammed, Napoleon, and Zoroaster.

———

"Although I would not meet him directly until years later, after the war's end, I actually had the privilege of attending one of Master Randolph's extraordinary demonstrations in New York as a skeptical reporter for a regional rag," the storyteller disclosed, gazing at the mirror.

His head dropped to his chest and he closed his eyes, swaying his crown like an opera aficionado contemplating an inspired aria.

"It was by far the most breathtaking experience of my life," he continued. "And that's quite an acknowledgement given my subsequent years as a battlefield reporter during the war."

The candle dimmed again, and the detective bent forward in his chair to better gauge the old man's expression.

"I reluctantly traveled from Poughkeepsie to the city to cover yet another alleged spirit master, far from uncommon in those early years of the movement. My editor needed a quick story on the latest in the field given the explosion of Spiritualism amongst our readership and in the northern region. He'd heard something about this 'remarkable Negro mystic' who could speak numerous languages while channeling the personas of prominent individuals who no longer walked the Earth. It was decided I would make the trip to see if the story had any legs."

Eyes gleaming, the storyteller poetically conveyed the event from his mind's eye, wholly embracing his own dramatics.

"There was something enchanted about that evening. Something surreal. The moon was satiated, a winter mist had rolled in from the East River, basking the city in a smoky radiance. I arrived at the venue, a sizable yet intimate theater by the water, at capacity, dimly lit. A few minutes after locating a spot to stand toward the rear, a spotlight intensified upon the circular stage, revealing an antique mirror. The excited crowd simmered.

Then, from the shadows, entered Master Randolph. At least that's what I foolishly thought at the time. But it wasn't. It wasn't Randolph at all. Rather, it was one of my childhood idols, the incomparable Ben Franklin. Certainly not in the flesh, given the radically unique facades of the two men, but very much so in the spirit, tone, intellect, and delivery given all I knew of and had studied of the man.

Reaching the mirror, this dark, large headed man peered deeply into its dusky glass for all of thirty seconds. Suddenly, he was overcome by three sharp jolts that left his diminutive frame trembling, entranced by spirit. His eyes rolled and he began speaking in a voice and style reminiscent of a prior century…"

The old man closed his eyes. His voice transformed.

> *Place an iron shot of three or four inches diameter on the mouth of a clean, dry glass bottle. By a fine silken thread from the ceiling, right over the mouth of the bottle, suspend a small cork ball, about the bigness of a marble: the thread of such a length, as that the cork ball may rest against the side of the shot. Electrify the shot, and the ball will be repelled to the distance of four or five inches, more or less according to the quantity of electricity. When in this state, if you present to the shot the point of a long, slender, sharp bodkin at six or eight inches distance, the repellency is instantly destroyed, and the cork flies to it. A blunt body must be brought within an inch and draw a spark to produce the same effect. To prove that the electrical fire is drawn off by the point: if you take the blade of the bodkin out of the wooden handle, and fix it in a stick of sealing wax, and then present it at the distance aforesaid no such effect follows; but slide one finger along the wax till you touch the blade, and the ball flies to the shot immediately. If you present the point in the dark, you will see, sometimes at a foot distance and more, a light gather upon it like that of a fire-fly or glow-worm; the less sharp the point, the nearer you must bring it to observe this light: and at whatever distance you see the light, you may draw off the electrical fire, and destroy the repellency. If a cork ball, so suspended, be repelled by the tube, and a point be presented quick to it, though at a considerable distance, tis surprising to see how suddenly it flies back to the tube. Points of wood do as well as those of metal, provided the wood is not dry…*

The storyteller quickly fell out of character and resumed.

"Though stunned by his riveting presentation and its authenticity, I became skeptical upon recognizing his recitation as the well circulated May 25, 1747 letter on electricity that Franklin penned to his associate, Peter Collison. Logic and my own arrogance quickly convinced me that this captivating Negro was little more than a well-schooled parrot, one who'd memorized the writings and speeches of a handful of famous figures, acting them out, albeit convincingly, on stage.

However, as the night unfolded, logic lost all bearing, arrogance transformed into awe. For Master Randolph—or whomever he may have been at a particular moment—not only proceeded to channel the demeanors, styles, and voices of several of history's greatest icons, he did so in their native tongues while their physical images miraculously materialized on glass, flashing back at him from the mirror's surface, mimicking his every gesture."

The detective squinted, cocking his head as if spotting a unicorn.

"*Exactly*, my good sir, wholly inexplicable. Mind you, this was no phenakistiscope or so-called 'Magic Disc' like the original picture movers spinning out of Europe at the time, not by any means. This was more in line with current developments in photography coming out of London today… Have you heard of Sir Donisthorpe's kinesigraph?"

Receiving a blank look, the storyteller continued.

"Well, you are certainly not alone, my good sir, for many have not. Apparently, an English banister has spent years perfecting an extraordinary little invention where a succession of photographic pictures is taken at equal intervals to record the changes taking place in the movement of the subject being photographed. In other words, this special photographic process recreates, then visually projects the continuous movement of a subject. It's simply exquisite. And from what I hear, our own 'Wizard of Menlo Park' is also doing some significant work in this area on the American side. But back to the matter at hand. Whatever technological or magical abilities Master Randolph invoked to produce such images a half century ago are well beyond my limited cognition.

Further, although I knew very little French at the time, after his summoning of Napoleon, the French contingency in the audience gasped with recognition. They later informed me that Randolph's delivery was flawless in its depiction of the turn of the century French ruler. Some were former soldiers who'd witnessed the legend himself deliver his April 1814 farewell address in the courtyard at Fontainebleau upon his failed invasion of Russia.

Still, it didn't stop there. For if it had, I could have chalked it all up to a sensational display of visual trickery, inspired acting, rote memorization, and highly effective training in language and speech. In itself, that would have been remarkable. However, Randolph then proceeded to engage each of his channeled beings from Franklin to Caesar in a spontaneous question and answer session with the audience, all in the historical figures' native tongues. These questions, I assure you, were not from planted members of the audience. By session's end, he'd answered questions from everyone in attendance, including yours truly."

The storyteller paused, then sighed, shaking his head as if the details were coming from his mouth for the very first time.

"By no means were these canned answers, but rather, full-fledged conversational responses to queries by a rich diversity of audience members ranging in culture, ethnicity, language, and country of origin. I had never seen anything like it, and I am pretty sure the others in attendance that evening felt the same.

After the event, a stagehand moved the mirror from the set to allow audience members to come onstage and meet Master Randolph face to face. While I certainly wanted to meet this extraordinary figure, my journalistic instincts, and the lengthy line forming, compelled me to slip backstage and locate the mirror to see if it would reveal some of its master's secrets. It was dark. Eerie. There was nothing back there except an anterior hallway leading to three doors, one marked 'Up,' one 'Down,' the third 'Out.' The stagehand was nowhere to be found.

Though unsure which one to take, I started moving toward the door marked 'Down.' Funny thing is, to this day I don't recall making that decision. I just remember moving toward it, finding it unlocked, and descending into utter darkness. Once I reached the bottom of the staircase, I could feel I was in a sizable room, uncarpeted, likely for the storage of stage props or other equipment.

My eyes eventually adjusted and were soon aided by a sliver of moonlight angling into a lone window at the top of an otherwise unmarked back wall. I could make out the mirror sitting by itself in the middle of the room, away from the various props lining the walls on each side."

The old man's eyes fluttered, momentarily breaking the focus of the spellbound detective. He quickly refocused.

"Even from across the room, it had what I could only describe as… an energy. A *presence*. As if something, *someone*, from its flawless glass was watching me, studying me.

I approached it slowly, and with each step, my reflection, dark, smoky, began to emerge. I thought it to be my own reflection, and it was, then again, it wasn't. I was somehow *different*. Younger, more vibrant. About seven feet from the mirror, I stopped and gazed into its pondlike façade, and… I saw… I saw… "

The storyteller's voice trailed, fell silent. His eyes fluttered once, then closed. His body went limp.

Realizing the old man may have uttered his last words, the detective snapped from his spell and rushed to the bed to check the old man for a pulse. He placed his head upon the storyteller's still chest, closed his eyes, and listened for a beat. Hearing nothing, his eyes popped open, staring back at themselves from the sizable mirror cornering the room.

CHAPTER VII

THE TEST

*P*aschal's gifts were far too extraordinary to go unheeded by those elite esoteric societies who specialized in cultivating such rare abilities. Not long after his New York demonstration, two French doctors in attendance approached the paranormal prodigy, praising his intellect and clairvoyance before inviting him to practice medicine with them and meet with several powerful people of "like minds."

Colonel Spear was first. Fresh off the Mexican American War, the mystically inclined military strategist, the Frenchmen reported, had been among the secret delegation handpicked by President Polk in 1845 to negotiate a compromise with Mexico, establishing the Rio Grande as the southern border of the recently annexed state of Texas. Given the instability of the Mexican government, and the lack of trust for their aggressive northern neighbors, Mexico repelled that effort, the hostilities commenced, the US prevailed in two years, and Spear made little secret of his secret role in the pre-conflict delegation.

Despite his title and the military regalia adorning his apparel, the massive, baritone-voiced Spear was an enigma, particularly due to his knack for speaking passionately, almost boastfully, about his increasing paranormal capabilities before falling silent for long periods of time, sometimes hours, sometimes days. During these extended periods, some believed him to be meditating with his eyes open. Others felt it was a heightened form of melancholy prompted by the trauma of war or personal loss. Whatever it was, it gave the six-foot three, 300-pound military advisor an air of mystery that, combined with his flowing white beard, unblinking eyes, and rich baritone delivery, compelled high-level officials to seek his counsel as if consulting Nostradamus himself.

Unbeknownst to Paschal, The Order had been watching him for some time. Like his French associates, Spear had attended the New York demonstration on behalf of The Order, a move prompted by ongoing feedback from numerous members witnessing Paschal's demonstrations. The colonel now sought to bring into the fold what he believed to be the most gifted prospect he'd ever observed. However, given the covert organization had a policy against recruiting, at least officially, the Frenchmen arranged for an exploratory meeting of the minds. So on the next full moon, a pleasant spring night in Lower Manhattan—geographically, not far from where Paschal was born, but economically worlds apart—the two men met. They sat alone in silence, staring across a large mahogany table at one another in a dimly-lit, Greek revival-styled interior room on the second floor of an imposing mansion adorned with pale granite ashlar, quoined corners, and embedded Doric pillars. Hundreds of old or rare books lined shelves on three of the room's four walls, the fourth adorned by a massive reproduction of Da Vinci's *The Last Supper.* A Renaissance-inspired chess set with intricately carved maple pieces centered the table between them. A small brass bell sat in front of the stoic Spear.

Finally, the massive man closed his eyes, took a deep breath, exhaling fully before refocusing on Paschal. He nodded knowingly; Paschal nodded back. Spear reached for the bell, ringing it once.

An elder white butler entered the room, a small black velvet box in hand. Placing it on the table, he opened it and retrieved a black silk blindfold. He positioned himself adjacent to Paschal, who nodded. The butler then wrapped the blindfold around the Negro's large head, eliminating all visibility and light. Paschal listened closely to footsteps moving deliberately to the side of the room, recognizing the *swoosh* of a book dislodging from its tightly packed position, followed by two more. The feet moved toward Spear, paused, pivoted, and exited the room. Pages flipped upon the closing of the door.

Though no words were exchanged, Paschal was well aware of the task at hand. He adjusted his shoulders and took three deep breaths before focusing inward, upon the space between his eyebrows. Within thirty seconds, his body began to tremble. A series of flashes and sparks swirled about his mind's eye, gradually giving way to a wafting white smoke dotted with strobing green and blue specks of light. Then it started to materialize. Hazy at first, growing ever clear with each passing breath. Relaxing his focus, a flawless image crystalized as if projected upon a large screen.

Thus, measuring things in Heaven by things on Earth, at thy request, and that thou may'st beware by what is past, to thee I have revealed what might have else to human race been hid; the discord which befell, and war in Heaven among the angelic powers, and the deep fall of those too high aspiring, who rebelled with Satan; he who envies now thy state, who now is plotting how he may seduce thee also from obedience, that with him, bereaved of happiness, thou may'st partake his punishment, eternal misery...

"... Book Six... Verses 893 to 904... Paradise Lost, Milton."

There was a momentary pause before one book slammed shut and another flipped open. Undistracted, Paschal remained in his trance, breathing through the nose, awaiting the appearance of the next image.

It materialized in half the time as the first.

Verum sine mendacio, certum, et verissimum.
Quod est inferius, est sicut quod est superius.
Et quod est superius, est sicut quod est inferius, ad perpetranda miracula rei unius.
Et sicut res omnes fuerunt ab uno, meditatione unius, sic omnes res natae ab hac una re, adaptatione.
Pater eius est Sol, mater eius est Luna.
Portavit illud ventus in ventre suo.
Nutrix eius terra est.

Pater omnis telesmi totius mundi est hic
Vis eius integra est, si versa fuerit in terram
Separabis terram ab igne, subtile ab spisso, suaviter cum
magno ingenio.
Ascendit a terra in coelum, iterumque descendit in ter-
ram, et recipit vim superiorum et inferiorum.
Sic habebis gloriam totius mundi.
Ideo fugiet a te omnis obscuritas.
Haec est totius fortitudinis fortitudo fortis, quia vincet
omnem rem subtilem, omnemque solidam penetrabit.
Sic mundus creatus est...

Paschal visualized then recited the English translation on a page adjacent to the Latin.

Tis true without lying, certain and most true.
That which is below is like that which is above
and that which is above is like that which is below
to do the miracles of one only thing
And as all things have been and arose from one by the
mediation of one:
so all things have their birth from this one thing by
adaptation.
The Sun is its father,
the moon its mother,
the wind hath carried it in its belly,
the earth is its nurse.
The father of all perfection in the whole world is here.
Its force or power is entire if it be converted into earth.
Separate thou the earth from the fire,
the subtle from the gross
sweetly with great industry.
It ascends from the earth to the heaven
and again it descends to the earth
and receives the force of things superior and inferior.
By this means you shall have the glory of the whole world

and thereby all obscurity shall fly from you.
Its force is above all force,
for it vanquishes every subtle thing and penetrates every
solid thing.
So was the world created...

...the Emerald Tablet... Hermes Trismegistus... Thoth."

Another pause, a book slammed shut, a third flipped open. The contemporaneity of the third image, and the similar racial makeup of its author brought a smile to Paschal's blanketed face who recited a part of the first line in flawless French before cutting it short to answer the unspoken query.

A peine arrivé au camp, le roi, qui avait si grande hâte
de se trouver en face de l'ennemi, et qui, à meilleur droit
que le cardinal, partageait sa haine contre...

...Les Trois Mousquetaires... The Three Musketeers... Alexandre Dumas."

"Bravo, Paschal, Bravo!" the baritone bellowed, ringing the bell. Footsteps quickly entered the room and the butler removed the blindfold, leaving Paschal beaming at his elated host. Spear rose; Paschal followed suit. Though the two could hardly present more of a physical contrast, they met in the middle and shook hands warmly as if they had known one another for years.

"I have one more question for you," said Spear. "This one verbal."

Paschal nodded in anticipation.

"Perhaps, you would like to meet some of my friends?"

Paschal was on his way. His engagements with The Order opened many a door and put him in the presence of some of the country's wealthiest and most powerful men. Many of these were northern abolitionists who recognized in the brilliant, clairvoyant, and eloquent young Negro a means of publicly advancing their antislavery agenda while privately satiating their own mystical proclivities.

Consistently, they not only supported his private demonstrations for their select elite brethren, but also his public lecture tours denouncing slavery while promoting citizenship and women's rights. Given his early nurturing by an outspoken mother, his daily struggle with racism, his desire to vote, and his growing aspirations for leadership, Paschal's promotion of such causes was at least as passionate as those sponsoring him.

For the first time in his life, despite his curse and race, Paschal felt largely appreciated for his mind, celebrated for his unusual gifts. However, it was more than that. Among the abolitionists and white elites who flocked to him after his demonstrations, Paschal detected in many of their wide eyes almost a form of *worship*, as if in the presence of a beloved king. They clamored to touch him, put their arm around him, interview him, and seek his intuition and advice on a wide array of the day's topics be it spirituality, God, politics, abolition, philosophy, medicine, marital relations or, commonly, sex.

Just as the western and central communities of New York state largely spawned the Spiritualism movement in America in the late 1840s, the region served as a bastion of nontraditional ideologies regarding marriage, communal living, and sexual freedom. At its core, Spiritualism was a reform movement encapsulating a host of existent expressions including equal rights for women, abolition, free speech, and *free love*, a generalized term characterizing a range of notions from the repudiation of "marriage slavery" to female sexual freedom to the existence of "soul mates." Such ideas were largely based in earlier concepts of the French utopian socialist, Charles Fourier, and promoted in the region by John Humphrey Noyes, founder of New York's Oneida Community in 1848. Characterized largely by its promotion of communalism and complex marriage—practices involving group marriage and the sharing of communal property and possessions—the Oneida Community was, at the time, far from alone in its rejection of longstanding institutions given the array of comparable state communities stretching from Long Island to Manhattan to the state's northern and western borders.

Meeting prominent abolitionist Gerrit Smith, Paschal relocated to the region as part of Smith's effort to resettle indigent Negroes on 120,000 acres of land he owned in northern New York. One of the wealthiest men in America, Smith saw in Paschal both a celebrated young mystic and an emerging player in his ongoing organizing of an antislavery political party, one formed in opposition to the apolitical abolitionism of William Lloyd Garrison and supporting his own presidential aspirations. While practicing medicine near Utica, penning a book on clairvoyance, and lecturing to promote Smith's politics and his own potential platform, Paschal became immersed in the free love movement of the area, exploring, counseling others, and partaking in its excesses. Though he'd later repudiate free love and his participation in the movement, the experience would ultimately refocus his promotion of the divine power of sex as being most effective between a man and woman in a loving, monogamous relationship.

After a three-month tour of Europe sponsored by Smith and introducing the gifted young mystic to elite brethren in England and France, Paschal, along with Spear, returned to upstate New York in the fall of 1850. Their charge from The Order was to grow the organization in America through increased lecturing, writing, and demonstrations around the country. The success of his European tour, combined with his rapidly rising star in Spiritualism at home, had wholly energized Paschal, and he now wished to capitalize by launching branches of his increasingly less covert organization in cities across the nation. With Smith's money at his back and the colonel by his side, he immersed himself in his new mission, touring the nation and opening branches while organizing politically for Smith's antislavery platform and lecturing on abolition, equal rights, healthy living, spiritual principles, and other issues consistent with those of his international organization.

Still, the mirror was never far away. It wasn't that Paschal required the instrument for his paranormal abilities given these gifts remained whether the glass was present or not. Rather, it was more of a relativistic phenomenon, a gravitational symptom, like the magnetic needle of a compass ever finding due north and, upon this cardinal sweet spot, the mirror acted as a tool for broadcasting and receiving images through his mind's eye, reflecting them on its liquidlike façade for all to see.

Late one evening after returning to his small farm in Utica from a lecture tour in Indiana, Paschal sat in his dark, book-lined den fronting the antique glass, eyes closed. A few feet away, Spear stood stoically, arms folded, observing every breath.

Although the colonel could not see the lights, flashes, and sparks beginning to course through Paschal's activated mind, he witnessed the telltale trembling and, soon after, the inky unveiling of two images on glass flanking the shoulders of Paschal's glowing reflection. Slowly, the images clarified, presenting two living men with whom Paschal was familiar, but had never met.

The first—40ish, pointed mustache and goatee, clad in bicorn hat, dark blue military tailcoat, ceremonial belt, and grand cross— was French president Napoleon III, the nephew of his legendary namesake who grew up in exile before being elected president of the Second Republic upon the Revolution of 1848. The second, also 40ish, saffron-skinned, tall, gangly, clad in ill-fitted suit with top hat, was a former congressman from Illinois, Abe Lincoln, who'd recently left the Capitol after one term to practice law back at home.

The mesmerized colonel withheld a gasp, immediately familiar with the images given his personal connection to both men through The Order. He'd briefly met the French president when traveling to Paris for his 1848 inauguration where a private ceremony was held to acknowledge the ascendance of this high-ranking member of his organization. Spear also shared an ongoing friendship with the former Illinois congressman who, when in the House, regularly invited him and other brethren to D.C. to discuss politics and matters of the spirit.

Spear was jarred from his recognition by what sounded like a female voice, less clear at first, then increasing in intensity with each repetition of the same name. Scanning the room for its source, he realized it was being channeled through Paschal, in trance.

Suddenly, it was crystal clear.

"PASCHAL!"

The unexpected clarity jolted both men as Spear gasped and Paschal's eyes popped open before collapsing from the chair to the wooden floor below.

CHAPTER VIII

THE PERFECT TRIM

*T*hough his mystical mirror was birthed several centuries before Paschal, its conception was rooted in the ancient world. Encased by the finest Flemish woodworkers in an intricately carved cherry wood, inlaid with ivory and staghorn, the mirror was fronted by a meticulously polished obsidian employed by Aztec priests in their divinations to *Tezcatlipoca*, god of rulers, warriors, and mystics whose name translated as "Smoking Mirror." It was brought to Europe by Cortés upon the 16th century conquest of Mexico before being shipped with additional spoils to Spanish king and Holy Roman Emperor, Charles V. Aware of the reputed mystical powers of Mesoamerican obsidian and its capacity to open an inky portal to another dimension, the powerful Hapsburg monarch had ensured his bloodthirsty conquistador included an ample supply of the ancient volcanic glass in shipments from newly colonized regions like Tenochtitlan, Pachuca, and Real del Monte.

The mirror, one of several commissioned by Charles, next surfaced at Mortlake in Surrey, England in the private collection of one John Dee. A 16th century mathematician, astrologer, and advisor to Queen Elizabeth I, Dee was widely recognized as possessing the gift of sight—the ability to see clearly through our Earthly veil and into the spirit world beyond. How the mirror got spirited away from Charles and into the sight of Dee is not as clear. Though Dee was certainly connected with the political and intellectual elites of the day, and friendly with Sir William Pickering, British ambassador to the Holy Roman Emperor, it was not uncommon for the booty of British pirates, some obtained from intercepting

Spanish ships bearing gifts to Charles' political allies, to eventually make its way to Richmond Palace, the favored residence of Queen Elizabeth.

Regardless of how the mirror got there, it didn't stay there. It next appeared hundreds of years and miles away in colonial America in the possession of one Ludwig von Wartenburg, a lesser Prussian noble, mirror-maker, and collector of rare antiquities. Knowing its fluid history, he had tracked the mirror from the private collection of a wealthy European family that had made their way to colonial America to worship on their own terms. Though communication was hard given his limited English, von Wartenburg had stayed in the colonies in search of a second, more precious and ancient relic, one reputed to have been yielded by the kings of old, back in the days before the emergence of Babylon and Nineveh, when magic and prophecy ruled, when princesses tempted suitors from lofty balconies, and when royal justice could be dispensed at the end of a sharp sickle. The obsessive von Wartenburg's life was devoted to locating the highly coveted sickle sword rumored to have once protected the Pharaonic line of Egypt before eventually resurfacing as a royal execution tool for an ancient king, egged on by an opportunistic vizier, and cursed by a doomed young poet in love.

Through years of painstaking research, the tenacious Prussian collector had mostly identified the path of the prized relic from the ancient to the contemporary, being retired from its employment as an active tool of execution before spending centuries mounted on walls of successive Holy Roman Emperors and national rulers, the most recent being England's Henry VIII. Still, von Wartenburg actually had no desire to collect the mystical weapon to covet or mount on a wall as some sort of ancient trophy. Instead, as a mirror maker who had now come into possession of the perfect mirror, he was looking to secure the magical sword to melt it into the perfect trim for framing its flawless obsidian façade. A practicing mystic himself, the recent immigrant wished to make the ultimate magic mirror imbued with ancient energies, a divine instrument by which he, like Dee, could see clearly through our Earthly veil and into the spirit world beyond.

The studious von Wartenburg had uncovered that Henry VIII was well known to have continued the Tudor practice of employing a "Groom of the Stool," a tradition of divine right placing kings on the level of gods and making it improper for a king to wipe his own ass. Accordingly, the Groom of the Stool, an ostensibly prestigious position delegated to a high-level aristocrat, was responsible for retrieving the king's toilet chair, administering enemas, collecting his stool for medical examination and, yes, wiping his royal ass. And few asses in the land were more royal than that of the blubbery, six-foot Henry.

However, Sir Anthony Penny was not your run-of-the-mill stool groomer. He had bigger dreams. Tired of the king's shit, the opportunistic aristocrat anticipated the instability that would follow Henry's looming death from an ulcerated leg wound and mass consumption of the royal buffet and, while others gathered around the bedchambers of the dying monarch feigning melancholy, Sir Penny quietly gathered the sickle sword from the massive royal collection at London's Whitehall Palace and pawned it to local pirates for three gold sovereigns and a one-way ticket to France. Once there, he established roots, a family and a lineage that would eventually see his grandchildren resettle in the Louisiana territory where they, in a desperate stretch, would unload the prized family heirloom to a local dealer who then rode north to Philadelphia to make a deal with an obsessive Prussian mirror maker named "von Burger-something" reportedly in desperate need of an ancient sickle sword to melt into the perfect trim.

Receiving a request by messenger at his Germantown location for a meeting at a neutral spot, the stunned Prussian immigrant became overwhelmed by the potential fulfillment of his lifelong quest to create the perfect mirror. Attempting to communicate in English, although not yet grasping plurality or tense, the flustered von Wartenburg scurried out the shop's front door, shouting back at his perplexed colonial business partner, *"Gots to go get me some trim."*

Granted, the trim he so desperately desired was at least a millennium old and had been mounted and handled repeatedly by everyone from all-powerful monarchs to stool grooming bandits. Nevertheless, von Wartenburg gladly paid a pretty penny for the ancient weapon before melting it down and carefully framing his looking glass in a magical bronze. Once complete, the anxious mirror maker waited for the next appropriate night to set up his precious one-of-a-kind looking glass in the dark alley adjacent to his premises for ideal viewing under clear and starry skies.

To his amazement, the mirror worked immediately. Five minutes into his first viewing session, a dark image slowly materialized behind von Wartenburg's own glowing image, growing clearer with each passing second. It eventually presented itself as an older teen, perhaps 20, with large puppy dog eyes and a vacuous stare. Then, the surreal specter began mouthing a phrase as if channeled from a different dimension, first softly, then more pronounced. Though unable to decipher the cryptic colonial delivery on the first two attempts, the third time was a charm as the voice suddenly came through crystal clear.

"Twere bet-her you jist give me the fhan-see glhass, Cahp-tin."

After all, this was Philly, and von Wartenburg wasn't from there. By the time he awoke the next morning, face down in the alley, clothes ruffled, and a bloody lump on his temple, the most extraordinary mirror in colonial America was on its way north by mud-wagon where its newly hired driver, a petty Irish street thug, could unload it where no one would care to look.

In 1827, the peculiar looking glass resurfaced in New York, appropriate, given winter that year was a strange affair in North America. It was a season of bizarre climatic anomalies producing extreme warming events or "false springs" in the East, including the widespread blossoming of fruit trees in mid-winter. This rare phenomenon prompted an unusually early opening of the Erie Canal to the north as the Hudson flowed free of ice, down through the city's southern tip, and along Battery Park. There, a Scots-Irish fisherman buoyed by the increased earnings brought on by the mild weather could now turn his attention to peddling the dusky antique mirror he'd won gambling at Coulthard's Brewery to uptowners in search of a deal. Or at least those willing to brave their way along Mulberry Bend to the open market at Five Points.

Things did not go according to plan. By day's end, the fisherman had received numerous offers but none he considered worthy of the fancy looking glass. Discouraged, he was just about to close his vending post when he looked up and saw the most beautiful woman he'd ever seen, toddler in tow, gazing into its obsidian façade. Like the mirror, her skin was dusky, flawless. Her large, lustrous eyes were like giant magnets for those who dared peer into them, even those white peers who considered themselves racially superior to the copper maiden. The fisherman was no different. Once locked into her spell, it was only a matter of time before the extraordinary glass, secured at a steep discount, was hand delivered by the googly-eyed seaman to her sizable home on Canal Street, the one purchased by a wealthy white property owner from an elite Virginia family three years prior, before abandoning her and the mixed-race baby boy in her womb.

Though she could hardly afford it, Flora needed the mirror. She truly wished to see herself in a different light given the pain of her broken relationship and the subsequent loneliness and poverty she'd descended into. Perhaps, with it, and her gift of sight, she could envision a different world, a kinder dimension, a better, more loving one to shelter both her weary heart and her precious baby boy.

The bright-eyed two-year-old needed the mirror as well. He regularly communicated with it, by thought if not words, nestling up to it, gazing into it as if it was the father he'd never had.

CHAPTER IX

COUNTRY LAWYER

*"**D**idn't think I was coming back,* did you?"

The detective shook his head at the struggling, slightly amused old man. He sighed, retrieved his chair, and sat back down. The candle flame shifted then intensified, catching a draft.

"Forgive me if I startled you, my dear sir. But I will repeat, I am not going anywhere until I finish my story," assured the storyteller. "Only then can the hounds have at me."

"I still had not met Master Randolph, although I kept abreast of his activities since we reporters have our sources. At the time—this would have been about 1850—Europe was still immersed in the unsteady aftermath of revolution, and America was in the throes of a gold rush and an escalating debate over the status of slavery for annexed territories. Master Randolph was living in upstate New York on Gerrit Smith's land practicing medicine, organizing politically, writing, and lecturing on spiritualism, abolitionism, and women's rights. His influence had grown considerably. Smith and his associate, Spear, sponsored and promoted Randolph in his increasingly popular endeavors, be it his lecture tours, paranormal demonstrations, organizing, or publishing efforts."

The storyteller paused to carefully consider what came next.

"Though, ostensibly, his political efforts were on behalf of Smith, who was subsequently elected to Congress as a Free Soiler, Master Randolph certainly had his own agenda, one based in his own political ambitions as well as his desire to break the spell of the ancient curse hounding him. Despite the plight of those who shared his darker hue, he nonetheless envisioned a day in a not-so-distant future where Negroes secured full freedom, citizenship, and the franchise. A day when he could further operationalize his growing network of powerful brethren and make his bid for public office."

The old man coughed hoarsely, before shifting gears.

"Miles away, in Illinois, one-term congressman Abe Lincoln had left public office in the Capitol to run a law practice back at home. During his brief stint in Congress, a term shortened by a year because of the progressing war with Mexico, Lincoln made little impact on the national political scene. He unsuccessfully proposed a fairly conservative and gradual abolition of slavery in the District of Columbia, subsequently bidding to contain the controversial institution by voting that all territory claimed from the Mexican conflict would remain free soil.

However, consistent with his Whig Party line, he did heavily criticize President Polk for the war itself on the House floor, promoting the conflict as both unnecessary and unconstitutional while clarifying the Mexicans had not initiated any aggressive or hostile acts toward the United States and had been attacked by the latter in a region which was rightfully theirs. And in a step that likely didn't earn him any friends in high places, Lincoln advanced that Polk should be held accountable for overstepping his executive powers by bypassing the Congress to wage war in the first place."

The storyteller stopped abruptly, recognizing his own propensity to detail significant national events as if he were the only one aware of them.

"Please forgive me, my dear sir, but there I go again. You would think that a man on his deathbed would get to the point with greater urgency. I am sure you are well aware of the politics surrounding the emergence of our late president."

"For the most part," said the slightly amused detective. "However, I don't mind the history lesson."

"Well, back at home in Illinois, Lincoln soon found out that his views against American expansionism were not popular, and that many of his constituents felt betrayed by his anti-aggression stance. As you know, Lincoln decided not to seek reelection to the House in 1848 as the Whigs lost his Illinois seat in the congressional contest, gaining the presidency with 'Old Rough and Ready' Zach Taylor. However, his legal practice flourished, as did his reputation for skilled lawyering and integrity upon navigating the state's Eighth Circuit and taking cases before the Illinois Supreme Court on behalf of manufacturers, banks, insurance companies, and merchants. Lincoln would later lobby on behalf of the Illinois Central Railroad and secure their charter before they retained him as their ongoing legal representative. He successfully defended the railroad company in avoiding payment of county tax before having to turn around and successfully sue them for avoiding paying his legal fee as well. Still, Lincoln was so effective as a lawyer that, despite the suit, the Illinois Central Railroad retained him again anyway."

The storyteller winked at the detective. "Not bad for a country lawyer."

The detective remained rapt.

"But back to 1850. Like most of us at the time, our future president was immersed in the debate over the direction of the institution of slavery in our increasingly polarized country. Morally opposed to the institution, he had organized and spoken out against it both in the Illinois state legislature and in Congress. However, as an attorney, Lincoln regularly had to prioritize his professional position over his personal views, representing in court both slave owners and those enslaved, be it the former seeking to reclaim those who'd escaped from their possession or the latter suing to win their freedom.

Sadly, right in the middle of his emerging legal success, the Lincoln family suffered the first of several extraordinary losses that would impact him deeply throughout his legal and political careers. It would also bring him into the presence of Master Randolph."

CHAPTER X

A CITIZEN NOT YET A CITIZEN

Although the toddler hung on for as long as he could, he was drifting farther away, toward the welcoming vortex of the infinite, far from empty, full of light. He sensed those about him, especially her, and though he could no longer see her, he still heard her voice in muted echoes, in prayers and lamentations. He still felt her touch, if not directly, in derivative perceptions of warmth.

His mother had always been there from the beginning, holding him, chasing after him, scolding him, teaching him, loving him, at the cottage on 8th & Jackson, built by the churchman who had married her to the country lawyer not so long ago.

His father was less present because of his demanding work schedule, but when there, doted on him, adored him, and called him "codger" while lifting him way up high to touch the clouds and soar like a bird on its way to a different place, one not so different from the beautiful place he now surrendered to.

Fifty-two days into a malady his doctors labeled as diphtheria, two months before his fourth birthday, Edward Baker Lincoln—more commonly known as "Little Eddy"—the second son of Abraham and Mary Todd Lincoln, was gone.

His parents were devastated. Inconsolable, Mary collapsed and stopped eating, eventually having to be forced by her husband to do so. She cried endlessly, remaining in her bedroom for days at a time as relatives tended to her surviving son, Robert.

As for Lincoln, already prone to recurring bouts of melancholy, he immersed himself in his legal practice to prevent his weary mind from spiraling downward toward the darkness, to the lair of the demons incessantly tugging at his spirit. The sun-starved hellions nagged at him to abandon all joy, seducing him toward a self-imposed departure from his current Hell to its more permanent counterpart.

The tall man was as peculiar as Paschal. Dark, gaunt, with massive ears, the former congressman and practicing attorney presented a profile more indicative of a reluctant attendant at a rural revival than a national legislator.

Like Paschal, Abraham Lincoln was a well-read, highly intelligent, and eloquent overachiever with a reputed penchant for dreams and visions. Like Paschal, Lincoln had lost his mother at an early age. Also like Paschal, Lincoln longed to connect with a loved one he'd lost.

Though the two knew of each other, and the colonel had befriended Lincoln more than a decade prior, this was their first meeting. In preparation for the evening session at the Springfield, Illinois residence of a high-ranking member of The Order, a sizable Italianate-style estate on North 4th Street adorned with bracketed cornices, cupola, and skylight, the colonel had briefed both men on the other's accomplishments, aspirations, and dispositions. This proved largely unnecessary since the two connected immediately as they gravitated to the estate's massive booklined study like tots to toys. By the light of a pair of three-arm French gilt-bronze candelabras, they recited their favorite passages from Shakespeare, praised the epic tales of Dumas, deconstructed the timely social critiques of Dickens' *David Copperfield* and Hawthorne's *The Scarlet Letter*, and recognized the ongoing relevance of the *Narrative of the Life of Frederick Douglass.* The discussion organically moved to politics and the establishment of the French Second Republic; the ongoing development of a viable antislavery political platform by Paschal and Smith; and related tensions in abolitionist circles between Smith's Liberty Party, Lincoln's Whig Party, and the recently established Free Soil Party of Salmon Chase and former president Martin Van Buren. They considered the debate over the slavery status of western states admitted to the Union, the looming Fugitive Slave Act in Congress, and the pending Fugitive Slave Law Convention in Cazenovia, New York to rally against it. They weighed the effort to outlaw slavery in Washington, D.C. in the aftermath of the Pearl Incident two years prior when 77 enslaved Negroes escaped the Capitol on a schooner named *The Pearl* before being captured on the Chesapeake Bay by a steamboat carrying an armed posse of 35 men near Point Lookout, Maryland.

While further acquainting themselves with each other's backgrounds, travels, politics, and passions, the two continued to browse the English, Latin, Greek, and French titles enticing them from all sides, reciting text or verse when inspired. An hour in, Lincoln fell silent when flipping through an 1824 collection of poetry by William Knox entitled *The Songs of Israel*. Recognizing the energy in the room had shifted, a curious Paschal looked over at his new friend, the one replicating the mirror's prophetic image, who peered intensely at a page in the book. The tall man's posture slumped slightly, his eyes narrowed and grew dark, glazing over as if entranced.

"Abraham?"

Lincoln's eyes jumped, jarred from his haze by Paschal's voice. Regaining his composure, he smiled wryly. "Please forgive me Paschal, but this poem… I had recited this for years, as a friend once recited it to me, but didn't know where it came from. It's my favorite poem. *Mortality*. I don't think I ever truly knew the depth of its meaning until now," acknowledged Lincoln, pain consuming his sullen face.

> *Oh, why should the spirit of mortal be proud?*
> *Like a swift-fleeting meteor, a fast-flying cloud*
> *A flash of the lightning, a break of the wave*
> *He passeth from life to his rest in the grave.*
>
> *The leaves of the oak and the willow shall fade,*
> *Be scattered around, and together be laid;*
> *And the young and the old, and the low and the high,*
> *Shall moulder to dust, and together shall lie.*

The infant a mother attended and loved;
The mother that infant's affection who proved;
The husband, that mother and infant who blest,
Each, all, are away to their dwellings of rest...

Voice cracking, Lincoln stopped. Pain reclaimed his angular face.

Before a mesmerized Paschal could offer a consoling word, the tall man quickly regained his composure, speaking evenly and wholly detached from the angst claiming his face seconds prior.

"I have these dreams," Lincoln admitted, his dark, motionless eyes focused on the bookshelf as if trying to read the contents of one of the massive tomes through its stitched rectangular binding. "Whenever someone close to me is about to die, I have these dreams. There's a boat, a ship, sailing along fast, and—"

Lincoln stopped abruptly, snapping from his trance as the colonel entered the room and nodded toward the two men.

"Gentlemen, the time has come."

Once again, the toddler was drifting. This time, the warmth and light consuming him was total, complete as a mother's love, clarifying his peace, buoying his joy. He was being beckoned, but unlike before, the voice was not hers. It was his, the one who'd lifted him skyward, made him fly.

Once strong, the voice now struggled.

"Eddy," Lincoln begged. "I am here, son. I just want to know if... if you are... in a good place. If you can hear my voice, let me know any way you can, son, that you are. Mama and I love you and we both miss you very much."

With Lincoln anxiously awaiting a response and Spear stoically flanking the two men seated in the dark study in front of the antique mirror, Paschal's body trembled, a symptom of the potent energies pulsing through his activated mind. After an eternal minute, an image slowly crystallized on glass above the glowing reflections of the two men. Once clarified, the playful voice of a child channeled through the entranced Paschal, echoing about the sizable study.

"Tapila!"

Lincoln gasped in recognition as the liquid image of his late son swirled into full view. Clad in a beige top with ruffled trim and trousers sewn by his mother, the boy grinned mischievously, swatting playfully toward his heart-wrenched father and quickly fading from view, channeling receding echoes of boyish laughter through Paschal.

The stunning episode left Lincoln glassy-eyed and shaking. *"Tapila*… that's what Little Eddy used to tell people when I was away in Congress, that I had '*gone tapila.*' His mother and I finally realized he was trying to say I had '*gone to the Capitol.*'"

Though Spear clung to Lincoln's extraordinary explanation, Paschal heard none of it. His body began to shake more violently than before, causing Lincoln to abandon his bittersweet emotions and turn his attention back to the trembling mystic. An agonizing moan escaped from Paschal's pursed lips.

"Paschal!" Lincoln called, to no avail. "Colonel! Is he alright?"

Unsure what to do, Spear stared blankly at Paschal. Finally, he took one step toward him, then stopped as if changing his mind. "Give him a minute. I think he's trying to tell us something."

Moments later, their attention was diverted as inky swirls appeared on the mirror, progressively unfolding into view and assuming the form of two soldiers, apparently identical twins. One was clad in a blue military uniform, the other in gray. Each stood on the remaining halves of a bifurcated land mass, facing off with rifle bayonets, poised to strike.

Beads of sweat dotted Paschal's glistening forehead while his eyeballs darted rapidly back and forth beneath their closed lids as if trying to escape his vibrating skull. A piercing yet composed female voice channeled through trembling lips.

Repeating a cryptic message, the image of the two soldiers slowly dispersed, giving way to the glowing reflections of Paschal and Lincoln.

"A citizen not yet a citizen will assist as you lead two nations into one."

CHAPTER XI

FACING SELF

*S*omewhere, *a clock ticked. At* least that was what Paschal sensed daily as he went about his routine writing, seeing patients, networking, and organizing for The Order and Smith's antislavery platform, along with his own aspiring political career. Although he had not made his future intentions known—and despite that most who looked like him could not yet vote—Paschal fully believed that at some point this wrong would be righted and the increasingly popular orator would tap into the support of wealthy white abolitionists and newly enfranchised Negroes.

For, ultimately, Paschal wanted to be loved and not cursed. He wanted to be embraced and celebrated for his incomparable gifts, not doomed by his ancient past or shunned for his dark, angular façade.

Nonetheless, a legendary curse still hijacked his dreams, waking him regularly, ever reminding him of his ancient culpability. And though he worked daily toward creating a world where he could rise above his current condition and somehow break the spell, Paschal was unsure how much time he had left, especially given his dreams were more recently and disturbingly followed by fleeting images of war and his own violent death.

Sleeping was a task. Like the antique mirror, sleep provided a realm where humanity's self-imposed veil was lifted, leaving the spirit exposed for what it truly was, timeless, formless, nonetheless imprinted with memory. The images swirled about his nightly canvas, projecting panoramically from his mind's eye to the room about him, consuming him in an ancient drama yet hinting toward the path ahead.

The border between Paschal's vivid dreams and his lived experiences was porous since he was unsure where one ceased and the other began. Even so, not long after their channeling session, he and Lincoln had concluded the former congressman was being prophetically summoned to reenter national politics and somehow, with the help of Paschal—a "citizen not yet a citizen" or free Negro—"lead two nations into one."

Though he did not know how such a dualistic prophecy would unfold, Paschal did know that the answer, the proper path, was somehow reflected by and contained within his beloved, accursed mirror. Similar to the firelit walls of Plato's allegorical cave, its shadowy images projected one version of a fragmented reality while teasing another, a higher level of existence unseen or denied by most, one unencumbered by constructed human belief and ultimately emancipated by its subject's relentless desire to know.

The young poet's eyes bulged in disbelief at his powerful accuser.

"Your majesty, I have committed no such act! I could *never* betray the hand of your daughter, nor the honor of your kingdom. I beg you sir, *please* don't—"

"*Silence!*" commanded the scowling Grand Vizier, stepping from behind the king's shoulder. Two stone-jawed guards draped in royal surcoats adorned with double-headed eagles flanked the ruler, their gold-trimmed insignia sharply contrasting the gloomy dungeon and the grim business at hand.

The king appeared conflicted by his captive's clear-eyed appeal. The vizier did not.

"After everything you have done, you dare offer his majesty more lies?" chided the vizier, attempting to sway the regent more than admonish the accused. "Have you *no shame?*"

The poet closed his eyes and prayed his nightmare would cease. *How had it come to this?* Just hours earlier, he'd enjoyed the happiest moments of his life upon winning the hand of the princess he passionately loved. The kingdom had honored their pending marriage with the largest celebration ever assembled, held on the sunniest day of the season, and attended by the most prominent families about the land.

Now, bound by neck and wrists to a cold-metal stockade block in a dark subterranean chamber of the palace, the young man stood accused of the unthinkable by the most powerful man in the world.

The king briefly studied the uncompromising demeanor of his vizier before taking a heavy breath and stepping dutifully toward the accused.

Desperate, the poet repeated his plea. "Your majesty, *please...*"

"Quiet, my son," the king interrupted gently. He raised his hand, placed it on his captive's trembling head, and closed his eyes. Mouth agape, the young man's eyes searched frantically for what would happen next.

The king's eyes popped open with purpose. He stepped deliberately from the accused, pivoted toward the massive guard to his left, and nodded.

The guard's approach was swift. By his third step, a three-foot brass sickle sword emerged from behind his back.

The poet gasped in horror. *"NO!!!"*

High above the guard's grimacing face, the razor-sharp sword glimmered momentarily as if kissed by a ray of sun, then rapidly descended toward the poet's immobilized head from whence came forth a final, tormented pledge.

"I CURSE YE ALL WHO—"

Paschal jerked from his trance, glaring wildly at the massive antique mirror. A lengthy, bifurcated crack adorned its previously unblemished glass façade, distorting his image into deranged segments. He didn't recall lashing out at the mystical glass. After all, it was not the mirror that was cursed.

Then he heard it. Soft, rhythmic drops kissing wood, diverting his focus to the deep crimson puddle forming below. Blood oozed from sliced flesh. Adrenaline gave way to pain.

A blood-seeping slit ran across his lower arm stopping just before its intersection with lifegiving vessels. Stunned, he pulled a handkerchief from his pocket, applying pressure to stem the flow. His heavy eyes returned to the mirror where, for the first time, he recognized blood oozing from the fissured glass bearing his distraught reflection.

The prescient glass was not done, for it had a story to tell. As the scattered segments of Paschal's image faded from view, another emerged, equally distorted, from the tiny, circular epicenter of the crack positioned at the center of his massive forehead.

Lincoln.

Paschal jolted backwards when he recognized his friend's image, losing his balance and tumbling to the hardwood floor of his dimly lit study. Rebounding quickly, his wild eyes again located the mirror, this time only seeing his own desperation staring back at him from its flawless, unbroken façade.

PART TWO

____

CHAPTER XII

PARIS

*"**H**uman exceptionalism is largely a myth.* Not only are opposable thumbs *not* unique, they merely speak to mechanics rather than to character or nature. Millions of years have done little to dispel the animalistic tendencies of human nature despite the extraordinary toys we have built. Doubt my words, do you, good sir?"

The wide-eyed detective remained silent.

"Well, if you truly want to expose the true essence of human nature, then take a trip to the most sophisticated and cultured museum or Opera House on the globe, be it the Musée du Louvre or the recently unveiled Palais Garnier in Paris. Seal and bolt all entries and announce that the first five individuals who make it out of the facility will live while the remainder will be subject to a torrent of bullets fired down from a company of soldiers manning the balconies, and see how effectively those opposable thumbs will grab, rip, gouge, and shred every last bit of human flesh, man, woman or child that prevents their escape."

The storyteller allowed the irony to resonate before shifting gears.

"Still, fortunately, there is another side to the long, ever-unfolding story of man, one depicting those rare, impactful beings be they prophet, mystic, revolutionary, or avatar, who challenge the perceived limits of our Earthly existence while redefining the realm of the possible. And if there ever was such an exceptional being, undoubtedly, it was Master Randolph."

———————

You have already been informed of the singular doom that hangs over me—that I am condemned to perpetual trans-migrations... How, when, or where I was found worthy of initiation, of course I am not at liberty to tell; suffice it that I belong to the Order, and have been—by renouncing certain things—admitted to the companionship of the living, the dead, and those who never die; have been admitted to the famous Derishavi-Laneh, and am familiar with the profoundest secrets of the Fakie-Deeva Records; and through life have had ever three great possibilities before me: one of these—I being a neutral soul—is that of becoming after death a chief of a supreme order, called the Light; or of its opposite, called the Shadow—to which I am tempted by invisible, but potent agencies; and the third of which is the one I dread most—the perpetuation of the doom to wander the Earth for ages, in various bodies, as the result of the curse pronounced by a dying man ages ago...

Doubtless you recollect that the curse was uttered by the young poet—and that the mysterious voice heard in the dungeon where he was slain, declared that thenceforth, until the doom was fully accomplished, this youth during all his ages should be known as the Stranger. Well, in the course of the centuries that rolled away, this Stranger became a member of an august Fraternity in the Heavens, known as the Power of the Light. You know, also, that I, who was the king, incurred the penalty of wandering till relieved; and you are also aware that him who was the vizier was sentenced to a singular destiny... he also became an active member of a vast Association in the Spaces, known as the Power of the Shadow... both knew that in my birth from the woman Flora—years before I underwent my present incarnation—that I would be in every respect a Neutral man; one having no tendencies whatever, naturally, to either good or evil, but only toward ATTAINMENT; and as such neutral man, it became possible to forego my doom, and to become supreme chief of either of the Orders named...

In one of my frequent sojourns in Paris... I was summoned to the Tuilleriés, by command of his majesty, Napoleon III... whom I had before met at the same place, but on a different errand than the present. What then and there transpired, so far as myself was an actor, it is not for me to say, further than that certain experiments in clairvoyance were regarded as very successful, even for Paris, which is the centre of the Mesmeric world, and where there are hundreds who will read you a book blindfolded...

On this occasion I had played and conquered at both chess and écarte, no word being spoken, the games simultaneous, and the players in three separate rooms...

The old man stopped reading, closed his bloodshot eyes, and placed Randolph's *The Wonderful Story of Ravalette* on his frail chest. The detective watched closely as his latest murder suspect, the one who'd implicated himself in a case closed 15 years prior, struggled to breathe.

"Master Randolph had passed every challenge presented him, had displayed his remarkable psychic abilities and mental acuity at the highest level and in the highest circles with the most powerful and capable of men," touted the storyteller, his weary eyes closed yet somehow marshalling his broken frame to briefly exude a semblance of majesty.

Upon a momentary pause, the old man's eyes suddenly popped open, cutting toward the detective like beacons piercing through the shadow cast by the dim, steady flame.

"Everything is Shadow and Light. *Everything.* There is the world we see, and the world as it actually is. Powerful societies of secrets operate at the nexus of the two, beyond the veil yet in plain sight, straddling positive and negative, the invisible and the visible, at least for those who know, those far-too-few enlightened souls who have cultivated the gift of inner vision.

Such a gift knows no particular race, class, religion, or ethnicity. It is neither the exclusive domain of the affluent or the wealthy, nor the celebrated or the elected. Though traditionally dominated by such groups, those born into a more advantageous lot in life, all men and, yes, women, can increase their station in life by cultivating their capacities for sight, for peering into the shadows before ultimately stepping into the light.

Master Randolph, despite suffering the relentless and daily plague of racism dominating our constructed American reality, was perhaps the purest, most profound example of such attainment within this eternal dance of shadow and light. He was well attuned to both sides of his dual nature and spent the majority of his existence striving to balance and reconcile the two, as is the mission of the enlightened, to return them into a unified whole, the divine state from which man entered our Earthly plane and, in doing so, arrive upon our original perfection as if for the first time."

The old man paused before driving his point home.

"Paris changed *everything*." He wore a slight smile. "Master Randolph entered the city mortal and left a *god*."

CHAPTER XIII

THE IRREPRESSIBLE CONFLICT

War has a way. It can start quietly, a barely discernible yet pulsing drumbeat, subtle as a beating heart, a phenomenon more felt than heard. Something within your spirit tells you it's there, tells you it's looming, even when your ears do not. Like a stealth Great White gliding upward to surface, it relentlessly persists, tilting its fin to enable greater pressure below it than above before exploding from its hydrous habitat to attack its prey. The latter is frozen by the explosive violence, though truth be told, somewhere deep in its spirit, the victim felt it coming all along.

Lincoln had felt the coming war for over a decade. It haunted him in daydreams and nightmares. He sensed a quickening as simmering tensions between the industrializing North and the plantation-based South had escalated upon the 1854 passage of the Kansas-Nebraska Act overturning the Missouri Compromise and enabling the expansion of slavery. The Act was largely promoted by a southern lobby fearful of the containment and potential loss of the institution of American slavery, its massive economic profits, free labor, and the southern social order it perpetuated. It had prompted Lincoln's return to the political stage as a Whig to briefly campaign for the Illinois House of Representatives before unsuccessfully pursuing the 1855 race for U.S. Senate. Despite his loss, Lincoln's stance against the expansion of slavery won him increased support among northern abolitionists at a time when the Act had galvanized them into further action and sparked the formation of the Republican Party.

A year after the Dred Scott decision further inflamed abolitionist sentiment, Lincoln would again unsuccessfully represent the increasingly powerful Republicans as a candidate for U.S. Senate in the 1858 midterms, an election cycle punctuated by New York senator William Seward's provocative characterization of the heightening tensions between North and South as "an irrepressible conflict between opposing and enduring forces" where "the United States must and will, sooner or later, become either entirely a slaveholding nation, or entirely a free-labor nation." Lincoln's performance in the high-profile Lincoln-Douglas Debates against Stephen Douglas—incumbent senator, colleague, and former suitor of his wife Mary—launched him into national prominence as a viable and compelling representative of a party that would dominate the midterms, taking control of the House and sweeping the northern gubernatorial races.

Still, yet again, he lost.

Then came John. Devout, dedicated, arrogant, fearless, loony, prophetic, compassionate, presumptuous, obstinate, delusional, driven, and as irrepressible as the ultimate conflict he was looking to ignite. Make no mistake, the War Between the States, the War of Southern Secession, the War for Southern Independence, the irrepressible conflict, the Civil War, or whatever other name a particular individual or region of the country has since chosen to label it was ultimately triggered by one crazed yet committed white man in 1859. While many to this day continue to dispute whether or not slavery was the primary cause of the conflict, few can deny the provocative role of staunch abolitionist John Brown in catalyzing the hostilities. Arguably, the first official shots fired in the American Civil War with the April 12, 1861 Confederate artillery attack on Fort Sumter in Charleston Harbor were *not* the first official shots fired in the American Civil War. That happened 18 months prior at a casually protected government armory at the confluence of the Potomac and Shenandoah Rivers where the current-day states of Maryland, Virginia, and West Virginia converge, in the tiny, lower valley town of Harper's Ferry, at the time a town with an apostrophe and located in the state of Virginia.

Like numerous prominent Black figures of the day, Paschal knew of John Brown and his outrageous plans well before they were set in motion. The incorrigible idealist had spent the years leading up to his historic armory seizure soliciting soldiers, support, and funding from Black and white abolitionists alike, among them Lincoln's private detective, Allan Pinkerton, who attended secret meetings with Brown in Chicago months prior to the event, giving him funds for clothes and supplies; Frederick Douglass, who rejected Brown's pleas to join his cause, labeling it a suicide mission; Harriet Tubman, who recruited former slaves from Canada to join the effort; and Gerrit Smith, Paschal's patron, who sold land to Brown and his family in North Elba, NY and a key member of the "Secret Six" who financially supported the raid at Harper's Ferry.

Though Brown's siege was deemed unsuccessful, Lincoln's political viability further increased as Republicans, abolitionists, and other pro-Union sympathizers were galvanized by the anti-slavery crusader's bold attempt, his subsequent execution, and his uncompromising commitment to emancipation. A year after the raid, the Republican Party prevailed in a high-stakes, four-way contest with less than forty percent of the popular vote but with a national electoral majority composed solely by a Northern electorate with a ticket of Abraham Lincoln and Hannibal Hamlin, two men with complexions so dark they were regularly characterized or slandered by political rivals and media as "Injun," "mulatto," "free Negro" or worse with their contemporaries commonly noting their "dark brown" hues and bushy hair as did an awestruck Walt Whitman with Lincoln.

Unfortunately for Lincoln, the electoral victory was the *easy* part. The President-elect still had to make his way cross country from Springfield to the White House *alive*, which he barely did. Uncovered plots to assassinate him in Cincinnati and Baltimore prompted an altered travel schedule by cover of night and triggered a subsequent press frenzy that depicted the newly-bearded Lincoln "sneaking" into the Oval Office.

Once there, the plots, death threats, and bad press relentlessly continued, substantially impacting Lincoln's dubious coronation on the brutally cold afternoon of March 4, 1861. Seven states had already seceded from the Union and more were expected to follow. A mob had attempted to break into the Capitol weeks earlier, on Feb. 13, 1861, to disrupt the counting of the states' certified electoral votes. Government soldiers and sharpshooters lined the roofs of houses on the route to the proceedings. A large number of special police combed the sizable crowd along the procession route. Cavalry soldiers rode alongside the presidential carriage, bucking their horses to thwart the focus of potential snipers. *The Washington Post* reported that government officials were "deeply concerned" that Confederates would shoot Lincoln as he rode in the open carriage with outgoing President James Buchanan. The *New York Daily Herald*, which had previously reported on the serious "attempt to prevent the inauguration of Mr. Lincoln, and perhaps to seize upon the federal capitol, by armed bands from the border slave states of Virginia and Maryland, aided by volunteers from neighboring slave states," summed up Inauguration Day 1861 with "Never since the formation of the government was an inauguration day invested with so much gloom."

Nonetheless, the heavily protected Lincoln would not only survive the inauguration, he would use his inaugural address to try and appease the South, emphatically clarifying he had "...no purpose, directly or indirectly, to interfere with the institution of slavery in the States where it exists. I believe I have no lawful right to do so, and I have no inclination to do so." Though personally opposed to slavery, the new president was a pragmatist ultimately committed to one outcome and to taking whatever course of action necessary to achieve it: the preservation of the Union. All else was secondary to this clearly stated goal as he equated secession with anarchy and vowed that the North would never initiate an attack on the South without provocation. Consistently, Lincoln ended his inaugural address—the speech his would-be assassins vowed he'd never deliver—with a conciliatory plea for unity:

> *I am loath to close. We are not enemies, but friends. We must not be enemies. Though passion may have strained,*

it must not break our bonds of affection. The mystic chords of memory, stretching from every battlefield and patriot grave to every living heart and hearthstone all over this broad land, will yet swell the chorus of the Union, when again touched, as surely they will be, by the better angels of our nature.

Better angels were nowhere to be found. Five weeks out from Lincoln's address, and a year and a half after Brown's raid on Harper's Ferry, the "Great Rebellion" officially commenced with Confederate forces opening fire on Fort Sumter, a federal facility in Charleston, South Carolina.

Lincoln's nightmare was upon him.

____

CHAPTER XIV

SOUL WORLD

Contrary to common belief, great secrets are best kept by thousands. Ironically, it is common belief that makes this so.

Since the dawn of existence, becoming God has been man's greatest quest. It is an endeavor only rivaled by man's relentless effort to prevent this process from occurring, an epic, invisible battle waged between the Knowers and the Believers, the former maintaining their privileged position through metaphor, forked tongue, and mass myth; the latter eagerly consuming these constructed realities, never knowing they are at war.

Nonetheless, if finding and becoming God has indeed been the driving quest of all of humanity, then hiding the Most-High must have been quite the task.

Eons ago, not long after The Deluge and commencement of our current cycle, not far removed from Zep Tepi and the return of the morning sun to the Eastern horizon, the Africans were the first recorded practitioners, carrying their ancient, otherworldly customs, traditions, and culture from the South along both arms of the snaking Nile from the Mountains of the Moon and the Land of Punt, establishing royal palaces, sacred writing, and Pharaonic rule at Ta-Seti in modern-day Sudan before reaching the land now known as Egypt and cementing their own divinity in the impossible form of thousands of tons of living stone, in sacred geometric structures imbued with mathematical precision and the spirit of the Creator. Though their megalithic masterpieces would astound, inspire, and attract generations up through our current day, their methods were esoteric, steeped in a longstanding mystery tradition passed down to proven initiates since the beginning of time, if time, in fact, had such a beginning.

However, whether it did or not, "The Word" was still The Word, manifesting itself in phonics, in language spoken into existence first in harder sounding consonants mimicking their cyclical cosmological origins and then clarified in softer divine breaths known as vowels. With such sacred phonics, creation and salvation myths abounded, all customized variants of an original, replete with colorful accounts of a many-faced hero, of epic sibling rivalries, of cautionary tales and dire warnings for those who dared touch the sky, dared peel back the clouds to see their own reflection, be it the destruction of the soaring tower of Babel, the fateful flight of the aspiring Icarus, the grotesque and eternal punishment of the humanity-loving Prometheus, or the epic expulsion of the fruit-foiled, knowledge-seeking First Couple.

Clearly, at least for those who promulgated such mythos, divinity was never intended for human consumption. Surely no establishment, no matter how powerful or consuming, could control such a knowledgeable and divine populous.

Not back then. Not now. Not ever.

The concept of church itself was a deliberate act by those in positions of influence and privilege to separate man from God, to maintain their own power despite their fear of an independent-minded, knowledge-driven citizenry bent on empowering and perfecting themselves through natural exploration, the pursuit of knowledge, scientific analysis, spiritual growth, and *sacred sex*—which was particularly potent and dangerous given its capacity to create life itself, a divine phenomenon triggering an all-out campaign by The Church to label this natural, species-sustaining act as *sin*ful while simultaneously deriving evil from Eve and relegating the Divine Feminine to a coded and metaphorical status only explored by esoteric societies of oath-bearing brethren.

For one such oath-taker, sacred sex was at the very core of his ongoing quest for higher knowledge.

One night—it was in far-off Jerusalem or Bethlehem, I really forget which—I made love to, and was loved by, a dusky maiden of Arabic blood. I of her, and the experience, learned—not directly, but by suggestion—the fundamental principle of the White Magic of Love; subsequently I became affiliated with some dervishes and fakirs of who, by suggestion still, I found the road to other knowledges; and of these devout practicers of a sublime and holy magic, I obtained additional clues—little threads of suggestion, which, being persistently followed, led my soul into labyrinths of knowledge themselves did not even suspect the existence of. I became practically what I was naturally—a mystic, and in time chief of the lofty brethren; taking the clues left by the masters, and pursuing them farther than they had ever been before; actually discovering the elixir of life; the universal Solvent, or the celestial Alkahest; the water of beauty and perpetual youth, and the philosopher's stone...

The old man stopped reading and tabled his copy of Randolph's *Eulis* to gauge the detective's demeanor. Seeing no more than a slightly raised brow, the storyteller turned to the second tome the detective had retrieved for him, Randolph's *The Ansairetic Mystery: A New Revelation Concerning Sex*, fumbling through its many pages before settling upon one.

Now, Man, being the chief work of Nature; allied to all that is; being the central figure upon which all forces play; and copulative union being the crowning figure upon which all forces play; and copulative union being the crowning act of his being—it follows that his moment of greatest Power is that in which Love unlooses the doors of his Spirit, and all his energies are in highest action; whence it happens that they who unitedly Will a thing, during copulative union and its mutual ending, possess the key of all possible Knowledge, the mighty wand of White Magic—may defy disease, disaster, keep

Death itself at bay, regain lost youth and wasted power, challenge permanent defeat, gain all good ends, reach the ultimate Spaces, commune with highest seraphs, bathe in the crystal seas of God's Infinite Love, and be in truth Sons and Daughters of the Ineffable Lord of Glory!

The detective shifted in his seat, brow bent.

"I beg your forgiveness, good sir, if you feel that I have gone off topic," offered the storyteller, prompting the officer to relax his posture. "I assure you I have not," he continued earnestly, eyes wide with intent. "You see, Master Randolph fully believed in the divine power of sex. In fact, he devoted many volumes to the subject, to love, to relationships, marriage, and to magic, which he ultimately believed that when effectively enacted, was its powerful result."

The storyteller lifted a shaking finger toward an upper section of the bookshelf. "*Love and Its Hidden History... Love and the Master Passion... Love, Woman, and Marriage... Eulis!: The History of Love... Magia Sexualis: Sexual Practices for Magical Power... Casca Llanna: Love, Woman, Marriage: The Grand Secret!...*"

He paused to acknowledge the detective's perplexed gaze at the bookshelf.

"Let me further assure you, good sir, that Master Randolph was not some sort of sexual deviant who employed his vast wisdom and unparalleled intellect to bed every mesmerized female who encountered his lectures, seances, or psychic demonstrations," asserted the old man. "To the contrary, he was a medical doctor who counseled patients and couples on their intimate affairs so they could live their best and most powerful lives, using the ancient ritual of lovemaking to improve their union and advance their spiritual gifts while optimizing their Earthly power and abundance."

Again, a reaper-like finger emerged from its tattered cocoon and lasered in on the spine of a sizable volume on the top shelf. Well accustomed to the routine at this point, the detective stood.

"That one, right there. *Human Love and Dealing with the Dead.* Yes, my good sir, bring it here."

Sex really means more than people even remotely suspect. In the SOUL-WORLD it does not serve the same purposes as on Earth. There, sex is of the mind—on Earth it is of the body mainly... Now let two such meet in the SOUL-WORLD, and if they are adapted to each other, their spheres—nay, their very lives—blend together; the result of which is mutual improvement, purification, gratification, enjoyment, and happiness—which state of bliss continues until new unfoldings from within shall unfit them for the further continuance of the union.

The detective's face relaxed as if the passage was more receptive to his ears.

Removing his glasses, the weary old man set the tome on the table and collapsed back to the bed. Eyes closed, his mouth pushed on. "Master Randolph, believe it or not, was a romantic who, toward the latter half of his brief life, advanced that the conjugal and sacred act of lovemaking between two committed and spiritually aware individuals, as opposed to random acts of mere lust, was a harnessing of divine power that could facilitate or greatly enhance the unfoldment of the soul, our latent capacities for soul sight or clairvoyance, the health and vitality of the loving couple, even the creation of more vibrant, intellectual, and capable offspring. He ultimately stressed marriage and monogamy as the ideal environment for such a powerful process."

Opening his eyes, the storyteller paused and searched the worn ceiling above.

"Sadly, Master Randolph's own unions were fleeting and far from godly. His first wife, Mary Jane, was a colored medicine woman who lived with him on Gerrit Smith's farm up in New York. They had a couple of kids together but I think only one survived childhood and went with the mother when their apparently troubled relationship ended.

That said, rumor had it that the relationship ended but the marriage did not, so when Master Randolph married again in Louisiana, he was actually *marrying again.* That is, without divorcing his first wife. Like the first, the union was rocky and brief and the white woman he married—some say she was Creole—apparently ran off with a free-love propagandist according to his own words. It did produce children and Master Randolph stayed in touch with them the best he could given his rigorous travel and lecture schedule.

His third marriage, here in Toledo—well, apparently, a marriage license was never recorded but we'll give Master Randolph the benefit of the doubt—was to a barely 20-year-old white woman, Kate Corson, a touring medium and businesswoman. Their relationship evolved from their work together as seers, and was troubled from the start. Their union produced a son, Osiris Budh, a year before that fateful day in July of 75 that has ultimately brought us together today."

The storyteller trailed off, eyes plummeting downward, ridden by guilt. Finally, he resumed, his tone more labored.

"By the start of the war, and despite his ongoing struggles with both the opposite sex and race, the persistent 36-year-old had managed to pen dozens of texts, launch and grow The Order, its locations and membership throughout the domestic arena, and assume the leadership over rulers, presidents, and other powerful members about the globe."

The old man's energy started to return. "Not only did Master Randolph accomplish these stunning feats, each one extraordinary in itself, he did so as a man of color at a time when those who shared his darker hue were still enslaved in a land that had brought them to its shores in shackles and continued to regard them as less than human."

The storyteller's eyes suddenly cleared and challenged the steady gaze of the detective. "Certainly, my good sir, you must admit that Master Randolph was, indeed, one for the ages."

CHAPTER XV

THE PATH OF THE TENTH

O*n a relatively quiet and unseasonably warm* April night in Washington, D.C., a strange gathering took place beneath the White House. It happened on the proverbial eve of war with the full moon traversing heavenly meridians and predetermining the spires of partially constructed monuments, nascent structures not yet majestic but serving as soiled temporary quarters for throngs of untested recruits clad in regulation blue, mirroring the electric-blue tint of the star-crossed city. Summoned soldiers, most not soldiers at all but small farmers and unwitting youth, had walked hundreds of miles to protect the city from the notorious "Wild Boys," those infamous sons of the South. The Wild Boys were at least as young as they, and hid about the city lying in wait to kill the recently-bearded Tall One who'd threatened their way of life, at least, according to what their red-faced daddies had told them.

The Wild Boys were energized by their newfound purpose, by relentless rumors of their sworn enemy's impending demise, distracted by such local drinking spots as Willard's Bar and brothels like The Wolf's Den dotting the rutted, unpaved streets and back alleys of the Capitol, checkered establishments also frequented by their opponents, be it the federal troops of General Winfield Scott or the private detectives of Allan Pinkerton, who had already thwarted an assassination attempt against the Tall One weeks earlier. They hated these northern aggressors for watching them, harassing them, and even hunting them while ironically sharing in the sexually-transmitted diseases brought on by their common intimacies and perversions.

Aspiring and established politicians, equally if not more perverse and diseased, were patrons as well, commonly cloaking themselves with false whiskers and aliases before exiting secret doors and back alleys, discreet routes prepared by the powerful Madam, to surface the following day, pants back up, front and center at the Capitol. There, they'd lobby the Tall One who, for the moment, was still breathing, and vie for a higher position of influence in a new administration sure to be doomed by war, dysfunction, and death, a much-desired and wholly appropriate environment for office seekers of their ilk.

Such was the pregnant backdrop on the eve of the great conflict as Lincoln, the reviled man with the fate of a crumbling country in his hands, slipped away from his weary team of advisors, presumed cabinet members, and security personnel scattered about the White House's second floor to make his way downstairs to the basement, into a sizable storage closet, and through its concealed, sliding back door. At the dimly gaslit mouth of a steep and narrow descending stairway he hesitated, closed his eyes momentarily and sighed, his emotions mirroring the encased flame's futile battle against the relentless darkness. Gathering himself, Lincoln softly repeated a passage from Milton's epic poem, *Paradise Lost*, as he proceeded downward into the vast, little-known subterranean network of dirt-lined, rat-infested tunnels connecting the White House with the Capitol, the Armory, the Smithsonian Castle, and the unfinished monument to President Washington.

> *Say first, for Heav'n hides nothing from thy view*
> *Nor the deep Tract of Hell, say first what cause*
> *Mov'd our Grand Parents in that happy State,*
> *Favour'd of Heav'n so highly, to fall off*
> *From their Creator, and transgress his Will*
> *For one restraint, Lords of the World besides?*
> *Who first seduc'd them to that fowl revolt?*
> *Th' infernal Serpent; he it was, whose guile*
> *Stird up with Envy and Revenge, deceiv'd*
> *The Mother of Mankinde, what time his Pride*

> *Had cast him out from Heav'n, with all his Host*
> *Of Rebel Angels, by whose aid aspiring*
> *To set himself in Glory above his Peers,*
> *He trusted to have equal'd the most High,*
> *If he oppos'd; and with ambitious aim*
> *Against the Throne and Monarchy of God*
> *Rais'd impious War in Heav'n and Battel proud*
> *With vain attempt. Him the Almighty Power*
> *Hurld headlong flaming from th' Ethereal Skie*
> *With hideous ruine and combustion down*
> *To bottomless perdition, there to dwell*
> *In Adamantine Chains and penal Fire,*
> *Who durst defie th' Omnipotent to Arms.*

A few minutes in, Lincoln fell silent as he navigated a long, dark tunnel lined on one side with a series of doors before reaching the thirteenth entrance, raising its gilded rose-inscribed striker, and clanking it down against its back plate in a short, rapid succession of patterned rhythms. Not waiting for a response, the man at the center of the young nation's most threatening conflict pushed open the door and entered a dimly-lit, perfectly-squared space where two familiar faces—one pale, the other browner than his own—sat deathly still, facing an antique mirror.

———

This time the mirror gave up its secrets more easily. Thirty-three minutes in, with Lincoln and Spear flanking the seated Paschal, the prophetic glass illuminated the dark room with its cosmic imagery. Flashing lights and shooting stars emerged from its nucleus and streaked the faces of its mesmerized onlookers. Unlike Spear and Lincoln, Paschal's eyes were closed, his head trembling and slightly tilted to the left. Glistening beads of perspiration dotted his pronounced brows.

The image was Lincoln. The Tall One stood majestically upon a raised platform in front of the Capitol on a brilliant, sunny day. In front of him, the land stretching from the Capitol to the still-forming Washington Monument was consumed by an earthen map, a raised, scaled replica of North and South. Upon the northern territory stood commanding general Ulysses S. Grant flanked by waves of Union troops saluting the President. High above, the colorful Union flag waved gallantly in a light but steady wind.

On the southern territory knelt Confederate general Robert E. Lee surrounded by downtrodden masses of rebel troops, heads bowed on sagged shoulders. The Confederate flag, tattered and faded, hung limply, half extended from its post, its tip dragging the ground.

The female voice pierced the deceptive veil of space and time to tease the future.

"Your legend will only grow as your life runs its course high upon the world stage, through the path of the Tenth."

Fifteen minutes after the session's end, amidst fan-shaped flames projected by gaslight, Colonel Spear watched intently as the two friends sat together to consider the promising riddle. Playing with several intriguing interpretations, the men concluded the Union was destined to prevail and that their global influence would spread to even greater heights than they'd previously imagined. The world was their stage, its inhabitants their audience. And while they could not figure out what was meant by "the path of the Tenth," they were certain it was a path to greatness.

Lincoln rose and saluted Spear, who returned his acknowledgement. "Well, gentlemen, I have a war to return to. Unfortunately, we cannot escape the responsibility of tomorrow by evading it today."

He turned to Paschal and warmly grabbed his hand. "My dear friend, I am humbled by your extraordinary gifts. I wholly recognize it must take a Herculean amount of energy and focus to pull back the Veil and see beyond our material existence, and I am truly grateful for both your vision and your friendship."

The President smiled and headed for the door before pausing, hand on the knob, and turning back. Sincerity bled from his gracious eyes.

"One day, Paschal, not long from now, I pray the world will openly celebrate your extraordinary mind as I do, will see you for the *king* you truly are."

CHAPTER XVI

PILLOWS VERSUS SWORDS

The castle sat at the end of the Earth, spiraling skyward, rimmed by mountains, shrouded in mist. Rather than some negotiated configuration erected by human hands, the massive medieval structure appeared as an outgrowth of its natural surroundings, a divine stalagmite formed from flawless stone and pointing heavenward as if identifying its place of origin.

For all its beauty, Paschal struggled to comprehend why a monument constructed to capture Heaven would straddle the pit of Hell. Barely a foot away from the castle's rear face, the Earth gave way to nothingness, a descent so jarring that anything more than a cursory look into the bottomless void could wholly disorient its viewer, coaxing them into its gravitational pull, never to be heard from again.

Queasy, Paschal wrenched his fluttering eyes from the ground floor window framing the endless abyss and adjusted his weighty crown. Today was not the day to let his fears distract him from the event at hand. Ascending the steep stairway toward the rear tower of the castle, the one directly overlooking the pit, the uneasy king recognized the irony of literally rising above his fear to ensure the marriage of the century was executed in the most flawless and majestic fashion possible.

The ceremony was one for the ages. His marriage to the wealthy princess of a foreign, nearly-as-influential kingdom was a cause for great celebration throughout the land. The alignment of the two royal powerhouses would cement Paschal's Babel-like domain as the mightiest regent on Earth with no apparent rival. Accordingly, the castle's facade was draped in brightly-colored tapestries, giant ribbons, and massive banners bearing the royal coat-of-arms, its windows and doorways rimmed with flowers and ivy. Prominent rulers and dignitaries from the four corners of the globe were in attendance, flanked by sizable horse-bearing entourages saddled with numerous shiny gifts. Commonfolk lined the lengthy and decorated entranceway to the castle buzzing with excitement, hoping to get a glance at the king and his new bride once the ceremony was complete and the royal couple descended the castle's spiral stairway back down to Earth to greet their adoring subjects.

Still, despite all of the pomp and circumstance, the glitter and gold, Paschal couldn't help but notice how precarious the whole thing was here at the rim of the Earth, on the edge of its highest cliff, a mere foot away from Hell. Adding to his uneasiness was that little was known about his bride, Dhoula Bel, rumored to be the most beautiful woman on Earth. Paschal privately wondered about this designation since to his knowledge, no one had ever actually *seen* the publicly-veiled princess who spent the vast majority of her days behind the high walls of her kingdom in a heavily guarded tower, far removed from the common eye.

Consumed by thought, Paschal moved onward, up the winding staircase, his flowing robe gathered at each step by the young boy trailing him. He came to an abrupt halt at a landing shy of his destination upon recognizing the beautiful melody that followed his ascension, reverberating from the surrounding stone, filling the staircase with a magical energy. It sounded otherworldly, yet familiar.

Paschal shot a curious glance back at the boy to locate the source of the music. No more than ten, the pleasant-faced lad smiled confidently back at the king and nodded as if wholly unintimidated by Paschal's powerful stature and fully absorbed in his own purpose. Like the extraordinary melody emanating from his vocal chords, the boy—who, by tradition, would double as his ringbearer—also appeared familiar, thought Paschal, likely one of his countless nephews who regularly bounced about the castle's centrally-located courtyard.

Nodding mechanically, the disoriented ruler thought to ask the boy where he'd learned that beautiful, haunting melody before dismissing his curiosity and resuming his ascent. After all, ringbearers commonly brought lofty feelings and joy to wedding ceremonies with their mere presence, traditionally representing matrimonial innocence along with future growth and possibility. In ancient Egypt, ringbearers commonly carried treasured jewels and ceremonial rings on ornamental pillows, a general tradition later particularized to weddings. However, during the Medieval Era when such elaborate pillows were rare, page boys did not bear rings since they were presented by adults to the betrothed couple on the tips of swords.

Pillows versus swords. The difference could not have been more stark.

Reaching the wide mouth of the tower, Paschal was greeted by blaring trumpets as all in attendance bowed to his majesty like birds pecking crumbs on the incessantly polished floor below. Moving down the aisle, he nodded majestically at the fellow monarchs, nobles, and dignitaries who had travelled great distances to honor this moment, or more accurately, to ensure their good graces and commercial relationship with the most powerful man in the world. Closing in on the altar, Paschal's heart plummeted upon realizing the decorative structure had been placed at the tower's edge, barely a foot away from the overwhelming nothingness that had shaken him moments prior.

Once in position, he feigned an authoritative look at his subjects before turning to cast a nervous glance over the far-too-close, rail-less edge. Before the nausea returned, his attention was drawn to another round of blaring trumpets, this time marking the introduction of his mysterious betrothed, the woman who would share in his rule over the very earth he currently straddled.

Face veiled, the bride-to-be was nonetheless stunning. Clad in an intricately-embroidered Egyptian blue dress expertly tapered in all the right spots, hair in a rose-petaled halo powdered blue, she paused momentarily at the mouth of the tower to nod at her bowed, soon-to-be subjects before gracefully gliding toward Paschal in a steady, seamless motion as if upon a magic carpet. Her obvious composure had the opposite effect on Paschal, who anxiously anticipated her approach, eyes fluttering in sync with his knees knocking beneath his garb. He desperately searched her unusually dark veil, an out-of-place covering further contrasted by the radiant blue surrounding it, for any hints of her facial features, expression, or much-rumored beauty, but the veil revealed none. Perusing the halo of powdered rose petals and hair crowning her head, the uncertain king's eyes dropped to study the tediously crafted design of rose stems that curved all about her voluptuous figure, thornlike prickles intact.

Finally, she was in place. An aged, austere priest, face long and drawn like a Basset Hound, assumed his precarious position between the couple and the pit, gravely nodding at the two as if wholly oblivious to the certain death skirting his heels. The ceremony began, rich, full tones bursting forth from a massive organ, its long, golden pipes climbing toward the tower spire, its thunderous chords filling the stone structure and flooding the senses of all those in attendance.

Except for Paschal, who heard none of it. Not the jarring tones of the all-consuming instrument, and certainly not the low, monotonous baritone of the priest who followed with a reading from a sizable Bible bound in rust-brown leather. The only thing Paschal heard, not with his ears but his mind, was the haunting melody of the young ringbearer, the jovial boy whose familiar face he could not place. The melody drowned out everything else, intensifying with every passing moment, with each ceremonial protocol. Paschal whipped his head about wildly to see if anyone was hearing what he did, but the faces surrounding him were as blank as the veiled woman to whom he was pledging his life.

Desperate, searching for a sense of logic, the monarch's eyes finally fell upon the only person who would return his wide-eyed gaze. Standing at the mouth of the tower, bearing an oversized ornamental pillow centered by two golden rings, the lad smiled at Paschal as if to acknowledge their conscious connection within a room of lifeless, unwitting beings.

But there was something different about him, Paschal noted. Somehow, he seemed older, taller, more mature, as if aging by the minute. His smile was no longer comforting, his brows hardened as if bearing some secret advantage over the struggling ruler. Despite the increasingly louder melody emanating from his vocal chords, now more aggravating than beautiful, the ringbearer's mouth barely moved.

Paschal could take no more. He spun around to command his wall-lining royal guard to grab the boy and put a stop to the relentless music, but they continued to gaze forward, looking past him with the same blank stares plaguing his attendees.

Then, everything began to spin as a torrent of images flooded his mind's eye. Paschal saw flashes of himself in another world, in another kingdom, in another time, overseeing a contest for the hand of his beautiful daughter; congratulating the young poet for solving the royal riddle; allowing the vizier to undermine the contest and overturn its results; issuing the chilling command to execute the poet in an underground chamber under the cover of night. Dizzy, nauseous, Paschal staggered about the tower platform, inches from its edge, clenching his head with both hands and violently screaming, "*Make it stop! Make it stop!*"

And suddenly, it did. The images halted, the melody disappeared. All that could be heard was the baritone of the priest as he pushed on with the ceremony. The attendees' faces, no longer blank, watched on with bright-eyed anticipation. The ringbearer, once again boyish and jovial, was making his way up the aisle with the pillowed jewelry.

Relieved, Paschal turned to the priest, who had completed his remarks and was now nodding suggestively at the new couple. Finally, Paschal turned toward his new wife, sighed graciously, and thrust back her dark, all-consuming veil.

In the place of her face, a mirror. Instead of his own reflection, a horrified Paschal came face to face with the grotesque features of the vizier admonishing him to execute the faultless poet. Over his shoulder, the glass captured the ringbearer—now fully matured into the poet—approaching Paschal from behind with a determined look, pulling a sickle sword from beneath the ring-bearing pillow. Terrified, Paschal quickly turned to the weapon-yielding poet before staggering back, past the priest, to the tower's edge.

Staring through the trembling monarch, the poet demanded, *"What three things are more desirable than Life, Light and Love?"*

Before the stuttering regent could respond, in one swift motion, the poet lopped off Paschal's crowned head and his dismembered body tumbled into the abyss.

Paschal awoke with a gasp, soaked in sweat, and instinctively reached for his head. His heart raced, his eyes searching wildly for the enemy no longer there.

CHAPTER XVII

COMING UP

*T**he conflict raged on. Two* years in, amidst key Union victories at Gettysburg and Vicksburg and unprecedented amounts of American bloodletting, the enlistment of Black soldiers by the North remained a contentious issue despite federal law authorizing their participation in the war effort a year earlier, in 1862. At issue was the type of participation by Black enlistees, be it as laborers or soldiers, and Paschal had recruited thousands to the Northern effort both for President Lincoln, who leaned toward their employment as laborers, and the abolitionist lobby, who mostly backed their deployment as soldiers.

An unofficial advisor and international diplomat for the President, Paschal had spent substantial time traveling overseas to rally Order members, particularly in Russia and France, to steer their governments to the Union cause and refrain from establishing separate trade relations with the Confederacy. He had also worked with members in Congress to compose key civil rights legislation that would set the legal stage for race relations in the looming post-war period given a Union victory over a struggling, undersupplied South now appeared likely.

On July 15, 1863, six months after the Emancipation Proclamation and less than two weeks removed from tide-turning Union victories at Gettysburg and Vicksburg, a state convention was held in Poughkeepsie, New York bringing together hundreds of Black New Yorkers by the Association for Promoting Colored Volunteers. The group appointed Paschal chair of its New York State Central Committee to further recruit Black men for the Union effort.

Four months later at a mass meeting on November 11, 1863, one week before his powerful friend delivered the Gettysburg Address, Paschal spearheaded the drafting of a letter to Edwin Stanton, United States Secretary of War, who ultimately approved federal pay for Black recruits. The Association then joined with the newly-formed yet influential Union League Club of New York City to establish a Joint Committee for Volunteers and recruit one thousand Black troops.

Despite the ongoing carnage, Paschal was in his element operating under the many hats of informal presidential advisor, war recruiter, global diplomat, and international leader of The Order. He was also an active touring author with the spring release of *Pre-Adamite Man*, a massive tome dedicated to Lincoln incorporating linguistics, ancient history, biblical criticism, geology, and paleontology to explain the origins of the human race. Given his popularity as an orator and author, his increasing power as a political advisor and society leader behind the scenes, and the likely postwar federal expansion of the vote to the country's Black inhabitants, Paschal's chances at launching a successful political career and breaking the grip of the ancient curse hounding him appeared more promising than ever.

His stock would rise even higher in the lead up to Lincoln's presidential reelection bid in 1864 as a New York delegate and leading organizer for the National Convention of Colored Men, a group concerned with the franchise, rights, and treatment of Black people in the postwar period. Held in Syracuse during the first week of October, the highly-anticipated convention attracted thousands as famed, formerly enslaved orator, Frederick Douglass, was elected president of the proceedings.

However, it was Paschal who dominated the four-day event with both his writing and oratory. On October 6, after spearheading the establishment of a National Equal Rights League and the drafting of a *Declaration of Wrongs and Rights*, Paschal set the gathering on fire with an animated keynote address invoking the divine nature of their struggle for equity in a country that continued to enslave them.

And yet his paths are plain. Let the nations take warning! God never sleeps. Wherefore let us all take heart. He fights our battles; and, where he fights, he wins. Wagner, Hudson, Petersburg, and all the other battles of this war have not been fought in vain; for the dead heroes of those and other bloody fields are the seeds of the mighty harvest of human goodness and greatness, yet to be reaped by the nations and the world, and by Afric's sable descendants on the soil of this, our native land. Be of good cheer! Behold the starry flag above our heads! What is it?

Eyes closed, suppressing a cough, the elderly storyteller pushed on through the memorized convention speech, his voice bearing the epic tone of a returned conqueror.

"It is the pledge of Heaven, that we are coming up from the long dark night of sorrow towards the morning's dawn; it is the rainbow of eternal hope, set in our Heaven, telling us that we shall never again be drowned in our own salt tears, forced up from our very souls' great depths by the worshippers of Moloch—great bloody-handed Mammon; it is a guaranty, by and from the God of Heaven, that we, the mourners, may and shall be happy yet...
"Here we are met, not to hear each other talk, not to mourn over the terrible shadows of the past; but we are here to prove our right to manhood... and to maintain these rights, not by force of mere appeal, not by loud threats, not by battle-axe and sabre, but by the divine right of brains, of will, of true patriotism, of manhood, of womanhood, of all that is great and noble and worth striving for in human character. We are here to ring the bells at the door of the world; proclaiming to the nations, to the white man in his palace, the slave in his hut, kings on their thrones, and to the whole broad universe, that WE ARE COMING UP!"

The detective nodded his appreciation at the old man's valiant effort.

The storyteller smiled weakly. "Because of Master Randolph's soaring reputation as a speaker, author, and political organizer, Lincoln asked him to travel to New Orleans, a southern city under Union control, to court the city's free, prominent, and independent-minded Black Creole population. Naturally, they recognized the potential political power at hand given the city's ten thousand free people of color and how a postwar alliance with Louisiana's formerly enslaved population would represent a numeric majority in the state. Because of this potential, the state was regularly the subject of the national press as it represented a pivotal political entity in an unfolding saga that would soon move beyond the fog of war.

However, as you may know, Louisiana's Creole population was unique in many ways. An exotic mix of African, French, Spanish and more. These Creoles were free, educated, often wealthy, and shared little else in common with the over three hundred thousand enslaved Africans manning the state's demanding rice plantations. With the advent of the hostilities, this unconventional group originally sided and fought with the Confederacy given their relatively good social status as compared to their enslaved brethren. As a group, since they still suffered the inequities and hostilities of racial discrimination, primarily the right to vote, the Creoles recognized their window for change and switched sides to fight with the North upon the 1862 Union takeover of New Orleans."

He paused, narrowed his eyes like a purring cat, and beamed them at the officer.

"Humor me, if you will, good sir. Do you remember Confederate General P.G.T. Beauregard?"

The detective calmly played along. "The Reb who started the war by forcing our boys to surrender Sumpter in '61."

"Exactly, dear sir! Pierre Gustave Toutant Beauregard, a wealthy landowner, West Point graduate, and the Confederacy's first war hero! And, of course, a Louisiana Creole."

The detective nodded in acknowledgement.

"Okay, good sir, now for the more challenging question, especially since we are both of the Northern disposition. What nickname was General Beauregard known by in Louisiana?"

Caught slightly off-guard, the perplexed police officer stared back at the old man, then a slight smirk of recognition spread across his face. "Been a long time since I heard that one, but I've spent some time in New Orleans as well," said the amused detective. "The little Black Frenchman."

"*Ha!*" The storyteller's energy returned solely to confirm the response. "The little Black Frenchman who, after the conflict, spent much of his time and wealth at home in New Orleans politicking for Black equity and civil rights. Right you are, sir!"

The two men briefly shared a smile.

"But I digress. Along with his official mission to help educate the free Black residents in the region, Master Randolph and the President hoped to secure the allegiance of this important but indeterminate bloc of colored folk going forward given the November 1864 reelection of Lincoln. Unfortunately for Master Randolph, there was nothing secure about his introduction to the state of Louisiana. On the day he arrived in New Orleans, still riding high from his much-publicized address at the National Convention of Colored Men, he rode a streetcar uptown to attend a Thanksgiving dinner with friends. Halfway to his destination, he was approached by a Union soldier who, apparently noting his darker hue, ordered him to exit the streetcar because he 'lacked the proper pass.' When Master Randolph refused, he was arrested and incarcerated in the local jail. That night, after countless protests, he was finally freed after offering a bribe, an unofficial $8 fee his jailers had come to expect.

When he was released, things looked promising, at least for a time. With his intellect, worldliness, and fluency in French, Master Randolph was initially embraced by the city's Black Creole population who likely saw their own elitist traits in this cultured Northerner. So much so, that not long after his arrival, his knowledge and reputation earned him an official resolution from the group bestowing the hospitalities of the city. The local Negro press celebrated him as a model for Black Creole children, as someone to emulate in intellect and literary prowess given his nascent effort to establish the first of the Freedmen Schools in New Orleans.

Unfortunately, as these Creoles interacted with Master Randolph on a regular basis establishing schools and organizing the January 1865 Louisiana State Colored Convention, his worst traits began to be revealed. With the early loss of his mother, his political ambitions, and his relentless need to be loved and celebrated by those he encountered, Master Randolph developed a habit of telling different groups what they wanted to hear without caring to recognize these groups might at some point engage each other."

The old man paused, eyes scanning the shelves. By the time he located his target, the detective was already in place. "The scrapbook, please. Thank you, sir."

Fumbling through a series of folded and yellowed newspaper clippings sticking to the book's inside cover, he continued.

"Mere months after praising the northern transplant, the *New Orleans Tribune* got hold of a critical letter Master Randolph had sent to the *Anglo-African News* in New York belittling the southern city's Black Creoles as 'a very small clique of very small men, whose day of power is already waning.' The *Tribune* reprinted the insulting letter, and at a community meeting on March 10, 1865 held at the city's Economy Hall, Master Randolph was publicly condemned in an official group resolution carried by the *Tribune*:

> WHEREAS, Dr. P. B. Randolph, representing himself as from New York, has abused of the hospitality and confidence of the citizens of New Orleans by writing letters to the *Anglo-African*, derogatory and detrimental to our cause, and said Randolph has thereby advanced Falsehood through that paper, calculated to place us in a wrong position before the world; therefore, *Be it resolved*, that we hereby declare that the said Randolph is unworthy of a place in our community; *Be it further resolved*, that we do not regard him as a true representative of the North."

Hands trembling, the storyteller folded the clip and returned it to the scrapbook.

"In true frying pan to fire form, Master Randolph left New Orleans—some say he was run out—only to end up weeks later in a rural Louisiana town west of the city where his ongoing efforts to teach free Black children brought the enmity of the Klan. Harassed, threatened, he wrote in his introduction of *Dealings with the Dead*, the book he was working on at the time, that each night he was 'obliged to sleep with pistols in my bed, because the assassins were abroad and red-handed Murder skulked and hovered round my door.' Such was the precarious environment of the day, so much so that Randolph helped a distant cousin, Edmonia Highgate, and several others found the Louisiana Educational Relief Association, an organization advancing Black education and aimed at continuing the learning process despite the violence faculty and students faced.

Sadly, they would face more. Not long after, over two hundred Black supporters of suffrage, education, and civil rights were murdered along with three white sympathizers by a massive mob of Klansmen, former Confederates, and New Orleans police when rallying at the 1866 Louisiana Constitutional Convention. Despite waving a white flag in surrender when exiting the site, the conventiongoers, ranging from schoolteachers to military veterans, were massacred along with additional Black bystanders by the heavily armed rioters."

The old man fell momentarily silent, as if to honor the fallen, then resumed.

"Even with these dire circumstances, Master Randolph managed to educate thousands of minds, young and old, while treating the area's infirmed with homeopathy and herbal medicines, some of them being indigenous to the region and come upon by his interactions with a local voodoo priestess."

CHAPTER XVIII

THE CLEARING

Everything moved but her. Above The Clearing, blackbirds swirled in formation, a massive, undulating wave of shifting shapes briefly forming a crown before transforming into a rotating vortex that, combined with the fall breeze, rustled leaves and excited the squirrels darting about the mostly bare tree limbs still feeding the crimson and gold earth below.

Then they were gone. Aside from Paschal's black boots crunching autumn's offerings, all else fell silent. Approaching her from behind, he was struck by her stillness amidst the floating leaves that descended lethargically about her. She straddled the mouth of The Clearing draped by a large red shawl, wisps of white hair climbing down the back of her copper neck from a spiraling indigo headwrap.

Although he could not see her face, there was something otherworldly, surreal, about her presence. Despite his steady approach, the woman never turned to look.

It was as if she already knew.

Nine steps out, Paschal swore the woman's frame dissolved into a blackbird before regaining form. He tried to steady his mind to allow his psychic abilities to inform him of what he had come upon, but he felt as if something was blocking his inner sight, a force stronger than his.

Six steps out, fear clutched his throat, restricting his breathing and pressuring his heart. Flashing images of the vizier's grotesque features and the determined sword-yielding poet flooded his psyche, positioning themselves in alternating fashion upon the unseen face of the motionless woman he cautiously approached.

Three steps out, the forest listened intently, conspired in silence as Paschal's anxiety swelled his eardrums and shut off his senses. He no longer had control over his faculties, drawn like a moth to a flame to his inevitable fate. His anxiety turned to horror.

One step out, Paschal stopped just off the left shoulder of the motionless figure at the mouth of The Clearing. Slowly, he reached out his right hand to touch her.

No longer able to take the tension, Paschal let out a primal scream, grabbed the woman by her shoulder, and whipped her around to reveal whatever supernatural horror awaited him.

A blinding flash. A crack of lightning.

The woman was gone.

Eh! eh! Bomba, hen! hen!
Canga bafio té
Canga moune dé lé
Canga do ki la
Canga, do ki la
Canga, li!

Steering the chant was the bamboulas. Driving, syncopated rhythms abounded, these African bamboo-drums jarring Paschal, then drawing him in, their gravitational pull part drumbeat, part ancestral calling. If nothing else was familiar, the popular New Orleans location was, the one locals labeled *"Place des Nègres,"* the sizable square dominated by Africans from Ayiti and Kongo and now illuminated by a large bonfire. Dark bodies leapt and soared through electric air joyously flirting with gravity, choral chants and shouts penetrated the cosmos and corralled the spirits to dance, to sing, to inspire, to guide, to speak. Their eyes reflected fire, both mirror and spirit; their movement—freedom.

Eh! eh! Bomba, hen! hen!
Canga bafio té
Canga moune dé lé

Canga do ki la
Canga, do ki la
Canga, li!

Most had been enslaved, some had always been free. They'd come from different lands, from Kongo, from the Gold Coast, from Ayiti, Cuba and about the Caribbean. They spoke many languages and they'd brought with them their culture, their intellect, their music, their ways of farming and eating, their rituals, their stargazing, their ancient systems of belief, their affirmations, their prayers and, inevitably, their Spirits.

Eh! eh! Bomba, hen! hen!
Canga bafio té
Canga moune dé lé
Canga do ki la
Canga, do ki la
Canga, li!

Paschal struggled to get his bearings. What was once The Clearing was now The Square. Gazing in from its stone-bordered mouth, Paschal's eyes were drawn, rather, *pulled* toward the center of The Square, past the frenzy, between the pulsing rhythms of drums, gourds, and jawbones, beyond bodies in motion, to the fire. There, the woman stood stoically, brows bent, staring back at him. *Through* him. Despite the intensity of the adjacent celebration and flames, heat felt by Paschal even at The Square's rim, her wide, penetrating eyes did not blink. Like magnets, they drew him closer, through the reverie, to the fire, until he was face to face with the majestic bronze woman with high cheekbones and a long neck adorned by conch shells and framed by dangling serpent-shaped earrings. Someone he'd never met but felt like he knew.

Her commanding, seductive voice, flavored by Haitian Creole, seemed to emanate from elsewhere.

"*Mwen pa renmen…* ghosts."

Trying to collect himself, Paschal stammered, "Y-you don't like… ghosts? I am not sure what you mean by—"

Her look intensified as she interrupted in clear English. "Your ghosts, Paschal! I don't like *your* ghosts."

Stunned at hearing his name, Paschal's mouth opened and his eyes searched in silence, but nothing came out.

"*Yes*, I know you Paschal. I know your past, I know your present, which is all there really is. I know your *future* as well," touted the unblinking woman. "Now tell me what you think *you* know."

Unsure what to say, Paschal remained silent.

"*Exactly*, my son," she acknowledged. "You know *nothing*! Once you acknowledge this, and stop trying to be something you are not, then everything will make sense. We don't do ghosts 'round here, Paschal. Ghosts are not of us, for we are a people of *Spirit*. And those spirits, *our* spirits, carry power, great power one might refer to as good or evil, positive or negative, depending on who calls them and what they are being summoned for. The ghosts that haunt you are the ghosts of our *oppressor* and they will continue to haunt you until you truly know who and whose you are, Paschal."

Temporarily forgetting the surreal nature of his environment, Paschal became defensive. "*I know who I am!* I am a seer who has pulled back the veil to fearlessly peer into the realm of the shadow! I have traveled the globe and studied with the great mystics of India, the Magnetists of France, the holy seers of the Orient, the—"

"*QUIET!*"

The sharp command was accompanied by an unseasonal gust of wind and the complete halt of the surrounding ceremony. Dark faces covered by intricate patterns of small conch shells and geometric shapes now glared at Paschal.

The wind subsided, and the woman composed herself and continued. "I do not question your accomplishments or your travels, Paschal. I question how you can travel the four corners of the Earth and still not know *you*. *That* is my question. What say you, Prince Jean?"

For the first time, the spellbound Paschal realized a striking, muscular middle-aged man stood statue-still a few feet behind the woman, staring intently at him. Without warning, the jet-black figure moved stealthily toward Paschal, his unblinking coal eyes as dark as his flawless skin. Identical scars mirrored his cheeks curving from the edge of pronounced temples to the corners of bearded blue-black lips. Sharing space on the beads circling his neck was a gris-gris bag and two small bones wrapped with a black string.

Flanking his summoner, the man spoke in third person with a patronizing authority. His accent, Paschal thought, sounded more west African than Haitian.

"What Jean say? Jean say you are cursed by your own prophecy and a prophet of your own curse. Jean say your mirror has two faces."

The soothsayer paused, closed his eyes. "Jean say you and your friend's current path—*the path of the Tenth*—is inevitable."

For a moment, all remained quiet aside from the relentless chirp of crickets. The night listened intently, as did a stunned Paschal.

Suddenly, the man's eyes popped open, revealing egg-white orbs. His body shook violently and he let out a bloodcurdling shriek. On cue, The Square erupted into celebration as if the reverie had never stopped.

> *Eh! eh! Bomba, hen! hen!*
> *Canga bafio té*
> *Canga moune dé lé*
> *Canga do ki la*
> *Canga, do ki la*
> *Canga, li!*

The woman silently commanded Paschal's gaze. She smiled at him as if she knew his secrets, all of them, his deepest, darkest fears, his many frailties and insecurities, even his ultimate fate. He wanted to run from the woman, from the ceremony, from it all, but he could not. His legs would not move and his eyes were glued to the mesmerizing scene playing out before him.

The fire drew him closer. He could not look away.

From the corner of his eye, Paschal saw something, *someone*, move rapidly toward the man called Jean. What had appeared as a trail of black smoke now materialized into a full-grown man, taut and muscled. The figure placed a bronze Grape Shot Revolver in the soothsayer's waiting hand before returning to smoke.

Though unsure of its purpose, Paschal's heart invaded his throat at the sight of the weapon, intuitively sensing that the outcome could not be good. His eyes bounced wildly back to the woman as if quizzing her on what was taking place. She maintained her smile while shifting her gaze toward her dark accomplice.

Before Paschal could scream, the man called Jean placed the gun to his own head, smiled, and pulled the trigger.

CHAPTER XIX

THE TRIGGER

"It was a decade of soldiers, rebels, martyrs, and villains. History is still sorting the difference between them… The godforsaken Southern rebellion had bled to its conclusion in April of '65 at Appomattox and the war-weary masses, both victor and vanquished, were uncertain what the future held after the extraordinary toll of carnage and destruction the country had endured."

Pupils dilated, the old man spoke as if reliving the conflict in person.

"The Union had prevailed. I dare not say 'won' given the massive and bloody cost of merely maintaining an already existing structure. Its controversial leader had been reelected and was already the subject of a mounting and indelible lore. Northern hopes juxtaposed Southern dismay in a palpable climate of uncertainty that—"

"I fought for the Union as a teenager," the detective interrupted with a nod. He'd been there for hours, and this time he was unwilling to play along.

"Ah, but of course you did, my good sir," the storyteller said knowingly. "You are undoubtedly a soldier. A brave one, I'd wager. Please forgive a pompous old man for speaking as if the most devastating conflict on American soil is some sort of coveted memento to be summoned for dramatic effect. I promise to do a better job of moving my account forward.

As a journalist covering New York's burgeoning spiritualist movement in the '50s, I had yet to meet Master Randolph although I'd witnessed that stunning presentation in New York. While his reputation as an extraordinary mystic and healer was spreading across the region, I had expected little more than the usual poorly orchestrated, smoke and mirror productions I'd grown used to wasting ink on. What I didn't expect was leaving the event that day questioning my own existence, my own purpose on this mortal plane. This unique individual had awakened something inside of me, something dormant yet powerful. By communing with those beyond the grave, his peculiar demonstration had somehow empowered me to see beyond my current notions of reality and even wonder if..."

The old man trailed off. The detective repositioned his shoulders, narrowed his eyes.

"I know this may sound farfetched, my good sir, and you are likely wondering what it has to do with an apparent case of suicide you closed back in July of '75. But I pray you keep an open mind as I continue my account. If you don't, I fear little else will make sense. I too was a nonbeliever, but..."

The storyteller stared wildly at his own grim reflection in the antique mirror cornering the room. The mesmerized detective looked on as the old man silently relived his first encounter with Paschal's mystical glass in his mind's eye.

The candle fluttered then resumed, as did the storyteller.

"The mirror was... something different. It was almost impossible for me to pull myself away. Even so, we would not officially cross paths until a decade later. Like many at the time, I was consumed with war, and as a newsman, committed to securing a front row seat to the unfolding conflict. Ultimately, I was privileged, gruesome honor that it was, to record the story of North versus South in ink, risking life and limb on more than one occasion before the conflict ground to its historic halt in '65.

I was glad it was over. Far too many promising young men taken, far too many families decimated. Still, the fight was so all-consuming that many a journalist who had clamored for a position near the front lines and depended on the steady demand for reporting to cover monthly income found themselves in limbo, largely uncertain of their futures as well as the future of our fragile national union. By then, I had already successfully lobbied to become a court reporter, and then a special assistant at the War Department under the far-too-powerful Edwin Stanton."

The storyteller paused, perusing his own grim reflection before his eyes plummeted.

"As anyone who worked closely with Secretary Stanton at that time could tell you, he was no friend of Lincoln. And with the pull of a trigger, everything would change."

CHAPTER XX

RIDDLING THE PATH

The first prophecy had come to pass. By spring 1865, facilitated by Paschal's counsel and covert diplomacy with influential Order members in foreign countries on behalf of the North, a weary Lincoln had won reelection, issued the Emancipation Proclamation, and bloodily forged *two nations into one*. Along with Colonel Spear, the three men envisioned a reconstructed South with full Negro citizenship and voting rights, a base from which the prominent Louisiana transplant could set sights on the U.S. Senate with Lincoln's full support.

In early April, while Paschal politicked, taught school, and made waves in Louisiana, the Capitol buzzed with anticipation over the impending end of the war. Since the turn of the year, with only a few states actively remaining in the southern rebellion, important events had unfolded that expedited the end of the conflict including the Union isolation of Wilmington, North Carolina; the capture of Columbia, South Carolina; the fall of the Confederate capitol in Richmond, Virginia; and Lee's surrender to Grant at Appomattox.

On April 14, five days after the courthouse surrender, the Union held a special ceremony to reinstate the federal flag at Fort Sumter. That evening, Paschal's dear friend of 14 years—the one who'd vowed to preserve the Union at all costs, who'd endured as leader over a brutal and bloody four-year conflict that took more than half-a-million lives, who'd prophetically forged two nations into one—did *not* want to go to the theater. His longtime friend and self-appointed bodyguard, Ward Hill Lamon, was away on assignment in Richmond but had advised the President before he left to stay away from public places, theaters in particular, given his concern over southern resentment in the aftermath of the surrender. But Mary had insisted, and Lincoln, considering the celebratory climate, thought the danger likely less than prior to surrender.

Even so, the President was more consumed with the recurrent dreams he'd been having. He'd confided one in particular to Lamon where mourners filed past a corpse lying on a catafalque in the White House East Room. When he asked a soldier standing guard "Who is dead in the White House?" the soldier replied, "The President, he was killed by an assassin." Further, that morning, Lincoln told members of his cabinet that he'd dreamed of sailing across an unknown body of water at great speed in an "indescribable vessel" toward an indefinite shore, and that he only experienced this dream before "nearly every great and important event of the War."

However, it would not stop him and Mary from unsuccessfully inviting Stanton and Grant, among others, to the theater that day; from traveling in a carriage that evening accompanied by a single Metropolitan police officer and guests Major Henry Rathbone and his fiancé Clara Harris; from arriving late at Ford's Theatre to attend the in-progress production, *Our American Cousin*; from greeting Ford's younger brother who escorted the presidential party up the stairs to the dress circle where a balcony box had been prepared for them at stage left; from taking his seat and unintentionally interrupting the play with gracious cheers from the audience; and from unintentionally interrupting the play again at 10:15pm by being shot in the back of the head with a .44-caliber derringer by Confederate sympathizer and the most famous actor of the day, John Wilkes Booth.

———————

Something shifted—energetic, if not physical. But something, somehow, was different. Paschal dismissed the feeling, thinking the matter at hand was far more important. Schools for educating the formerly enslaved were popping up about the state at a rapid pace, and by April '65 these mission-driven institutions were being prepared for consolidation under the Bureau of Refugees, Freedmen, and Abandoned Lands established a month prior by the federal government. Due to his representation of the office of the President and his tireless drive to promote education in New Orleans and throughout the surrounding communities, his own role in the process had been substantial, keeping him in constant demand as a paid speaker.

Needing both the money and the attention, Paschal made his way on the afternoon of April 15 to the city's latest school to open as he was slated to deliver the keynote address. Rounding the facility's brick corner, he was thrilled to see his own name and image plastered on paper ads adorning the school's façade.

Then, he saw him, first from the corner of his eye, poised, waiting. Paschal's heart lodged in his throat upon coming face to face with the Union soldier who'd arrested him on the streetcar his first day in New Orleans.

"Well, well, well." The soldier smiled, his eyes cutting through Paschal's stunned gaze. "If it isn't *Mister Uppity Northern Negro* himself. Heard you got a big, important speech today, *Mister Uppity.* Got your face plastered all over town. Wow, just look at you."

Nervous, Paschal remained silent.

"Now you wouldn't be trying to rile up our southern darkies with all your fancified northern knowledge, would ya? *Huh?*" Animated, the soldier continued his roleplay. "And I don't remember getting *my* invitation. Were you planning on inviting me?"

Paschal struggled to compose himself. "I… I didn't think this was your type of crowd… sir. "

"Oh *contrare*, Mister Uppity! You are wrong, so very wrong! For this is *exactly* the kind of crowd I need to be around. *Dark, gullible* and *uppity.* Yep, that's my place alright, ensuring that the likes of you don't put any more of them uppity ideas into the heads of our local niggers. They just *fine* the way they are, thank you very much!"

Unsure how to respond, Paschal stared blankly at the narrow-eyed soldier with the faux smile before cautiously maneuvering around him and entering the building.

———

Despite his building-side encounter, the speech went well… until it didn't. Halfway through, Paschal was in full command of the audience, passionately invoking the struggles of their collective past, animatedly relaying the promise of the present moment, and excitedly teasing the potentialities of the future when, from the corner of his eye, he caught an elderly woman slowly making her way down a side aisle toward the stage. She was bearing a stunned, out-of-place expression, eyes red and wide, mouth hanging open as she pressed on. Not wanting to break his focus, Paschal attempted to push her image from his mind and maintain the energy of his address but there was something about her gaze that would not allow him to, especially since this was the same woman he'd seen a mere hour before tending to the administrators who bustled about the school's main office. Then, the receptionist had appeared confident and efficient, someone who already well new her role within the functioning of the new institution. However, she now seemed frail and disillusioned as if suddenly struck with dementia or some other crippling cognitive ailment.

And then, mid-speech, hypnotized by the mesmerizing, steady pace of the woman's steps against the blaring silence of the audience, it came crashing back. The Shift was upon him once more and space and time collapsed back into the aether, the teeming black medium that spawned it, beyond past, present, and future and into its infinite, all-knowing source. There, he saw a boat—or what appeared to be a boat—clothed in several coats of the finest white paint, hovering more than drifting on a clear, mostly still aqua blue sea. Before Paschal knew it, he was upon it, gliding, soaring effortlessly at a great speed across this vast unknown body of water toward what he believed to be a distant shore.

In front of him, consuming much of the vessel's interior, was an oversized white coffin trimmed in gold. The sun sparkled about its brilliant exterior.

Instinctively, a curious Paschal studied its flawless casing in search of a latch. He needed to know who was buried inside. Running his fingers under the casket's left lip, Paschal located a golden latch and pulled until he heard a click. He tugged at the surprisingly light door before raising it halfway and—

Paschal snapped from his trance when the receptionist unleashed a bloodcurdling scream that jolted the audience. Voices questioned, eyes searched, then fell upon the distraught woman.

Her next words, shouted in distress, brought a collective gasp that sucked the air from the building.

"Somebody done killed the President! Oh God! Somebody done killed President Lincoln!"

Stunned, Paschal's eyes searched for meaning while audience members reeled in shock, grabbing their own faces or clutching the nearest arm of their neighbor. Some spoke animatedly, begging to know if it the news was true. Others cried out in anguish. As the cacophony reached a crescendo, Paschal shook off his stupor and left the podium to approach the receptionist about her bizarre statement. As far as he was concerned, the news could not be true for the war was over, the South had surrendered, and his dear friend had been re-elected to a second term. Lincoln had survived the greatest conflict in the country's history, so he certainly would survive the peace, Paschal reasoned. The woman was delusional at most, misinformed at least.

Closing in on the weeping woman, Paschal saw she clutched a rolled-up newspaper in her hand. When they were finally face to face, the woman ceased sobbing and stared wildly into Paschal's searching eyes. He held out his hand and the woman complied, reluctantly placing in it a copy of the day's *Tribune*. Without breaking eye contact, Paschal slowly unrolled the paper as if his pace could buy him more time to get his bearings, better prepare him for any trauma it might present.

It did not. A minute later, Paschal was on his knees clutching his stomach, eyes wide open, seeing nothing. The image of Lincoln's stoic, weathered face stared up at him.

Ten minutes later, like the remaining audience members, Paschal was deeply engrossed in the paper's vivid description of the assassination and its key players. After reading the full account, the distraught Northerner came to grips with the forked truth of prophecy, that the President's life had *run its course* in the balcony high above the world-renowned stage at Ford's Theatre before being moved, mostly dead, across *the path of the Tenth* to the Peterson Boarding House at 516 10th Street Northwest where he succumbed the next morning.

CHAPTER XXI

ENEMIES WITHIN

*"T*he thing about enemies is* that they are ultimately a reflection of ourselves." The old man peered at the mirror again, flirting with soliloquy. "They are the physical embodiment or manifestation of our insecurities and fears, be they real or imagined. And contrary to popular opinion, enemies are not our opposition; rather, enemies are *ourselves*, staring back at us, reflecting parts of us we deny or don't wish to acknowledge. Enemies are a mirror playing out in full form, in real time, haunting us, cajoling us, challenging us to face what we have been frightened into avoiding.

Lincoln certainly had his enemies, near and far. They lined his presidential cabinet and composed the rank and file of the Confederacy. They resided in lofty places, from the competing esoteric societies of business magnates and global leaders to the soaring, arched corridors of the Vatican. They had a variety of motives and incentives to see the demise of Lincoln, mostly pertaining to the course of the nation, its economics, and its system of banking. And particularly its politics, namely, how the decimated South would figure into a postwar world and who should rule over such a powerful, reemerging, and globally strategic entity."

The storyteller paused, his gaze returning to the detective. "The thing about power is, the more you crave it, the more you push to accumulate it. Yet the more you accumulate it, the more you crave it."

"Secretary Stanton was a powerful man. My years under him at the War Department gave me a front row view of his stunning authority and reach. He was a relentless political operative whose thirst for power was as strong as Lincoln's desire to keep the Union intact. In the postwar phase, Stanton was dead set on punishing the South for their rebellion and, in the process, extracting the wealth from the region in the form of plantation cotton profits and other lucrative crops the South produced. Indeed, Stanton was bent on enacting a far more radical policy of Reconstruction that crippled the South, commandeered its primary revenue streams, modified the system of banking, and greatly increased his own influence given the War Department's active role in such a process.

Lincoln opposed this course of action and strongly favored a high-road approach to Reconstruction, desiring to resurrect the Union with a more amicable reincorporation of the South."

The old man fell quiet and contemplated the encroaching ceiling. He shifted slightly on his perch. Then he asked, "How much do you know about the Peterson House?"

The detective's eyes searched momentarily before rebounding. "The place where Lincoln died?"

"*Yes*, my good sir. The boarding house containing the room where our 16th president took his last breath. If you recall, the Peterson House across from Ford's Theatre in Washington initially received quite a bit of national attention in the aftermath of the assassination as thousands flocked to see where Lincoln left this world, to feel his lingering presence, to photograph the location, even to steal and market bits and pieces of the room's carpet, furniture, and any other remaining items. But what has been given less attention are the inhabitants of the house itself."

Brow bent, the detective tilted his head.

"You may recall, sir, that after Lincoln was shot, he was carried by a group of men, including physicians, out of the theater and onto the street. One Henry Safford, a boarder at the Peterson House, then persuaded them to bring the grievously wounded president there, to a bedroom at the back of the house rented out by another man, Willie Clark. Clark was not at home as the men accessed the open room and continued attending to the president."

Eyes plummeting, the storyteller perused the tattered blanket mummifying him. This time, they remained there.

"What folks often fail to mention is that Clark and Safford, along with another boarder there, Thomas Proctor, all worked for Stanton at the War Department. That's not necessarily an important detail since many residents in that area worked under Stanton at the time, especially since the nation was at war. In fact, I, myself, worked with each of these men in one capacity or another during my tenure at the Department."

His voice trailed, lost in thought. After a pregnant minute, he resumed.

"What folks also fail to mention is that several actors from Ford's Theatre also lived there, including Charles Warwick and John Matthews. Again, not necessarily a significant detail given the popular theater is located right across from the house."

The detective was blunt. "Where are you going with this?"

The cop's straightforward demeanor jarred the old man's eyes from the floor.

"My apologies for contemplating out loud, my good sir, but don't you find it a bit fascinating that a substantial segment, actually half of the boarders at the Peterson House, were either working with Stanton and me at the War Department or with Ford's Theatre? That our unconscious president, given Booth's failure to finish the job at the theater, was *steered* to the Peterson House by a member of the War Department? That the room he was brought to and ultimately died in was rented out by another member of the War Department?"

The storyteller's tone gained gravity.

"That in this *very same room*, mere weeks before the assassination, the actor Charles Matthews was visited by none other than his good friend and fellow actor, the assassin himself, John Wilkes Booth?"

The detective's rigid demeanor faltered, unable to conceal his bewilderment.

"Yes, sir," the old man nodded in confirmation. "You heard me correctly. In fact, Henry Safford recently, upon the anniversary of the shooting at Ford's, submitted a lengthy press statement on the events surrounding the assassination, acknowledging this. But by no means do such *fascinating* events and relationships end there.

Were you aware that Lincoln's successor, Andrew Johnson, and John Wilkes Booth were longtime acquaintances, so much so that they actually were intimately involved with a pair of sisters back in Tennessee, well before the murder of Lincoln? That on the afternoon of April 14, hours before he shot the President, Booth left a calling card for then Vice President Johnson, who was staying at the Kirkwood Hotel, that read, *'Don't wish to disturb you... Are you at home? J. Wilkes Booth.'*

Booth had received a large amount of money from a northern bank to which Stanton was well connected, weeks before the assassination. Did you know that? Or that Stanton denied Lincoln's request to be accompanied and protected by Major Thomas Eckert at Ford's, and despite numerous death threats, sent only one bodyguard to the theater that night who famously abandoned his post prior to the shooting yet was never held accountable for his actions afterwards by Stanton or any other government entity?"

The storyteller paused to catch his breath, then continued.

"That after the shooting, Stanton ordered the military to close off seven of the eight escape routes leading out of Washington, every route *except* for the one taken by Booth? Or did you know that on the night of the assassination, telegraph lines in the city controlled by the War Department went dead, thereby delaying the news of Booth's escape? Or that Colonel Lafayette Baker, head of the National Detective Bureau, Stanton's top spy, and the man most credited with tracking down Booth after the assassination—despite much evidence the assassin remains alive today—subsequently testified before Congress and implicated himself and Stanton as part of a larger plot to kill Lincoln?

After his testimony, Baker openly feared for his life, saying that Stanton would have him poisoned. He mysteriously fell dead not long after, the official cause being labeled as *meningitis*."

Anguish suddenly consumed the old man's face.

"Did you know...that... that... that..."

The stutter broke the spell the detective was under just before the storyteller's body went limp and tumbled lifeless from bed to floor.

CHAPTER XXII

THE TRAIN

*T*he *Nigger had to go.* He did not belong. Not now, not on an important occasion like this. Several members of the procession had questioned his troubling copper hue and subsequently his presence as the decorated locomotive churned westward through the open countryside on its somber, 1666-mile journey toward Springfield, the final resting place of the fallen, the site the deceased called home.

It was certainly not the first time Paschal had endured the heat of racial scrutiny. Perplexed squints gave way to wide-eyed suspicion before succumbing to an agitated acknowledgement that something was wrong, was out of place. Despite all his learning, the medical title preceding his name, the formative role his family played in the establishment of the New World, and his leadership of an esoteric society of some of the world's most powerful men including the deceased, *he* was that troubling, out-of-place something. No accomplishments, no matter how prestigious or numerous, could prevent his expulsion. No passing reference to his worldwide travels or to the numerous kings and world leaders he advised, entertained or counseled would suffice. To the already emotional passengers riding the train that grave spring day, he was just a nigger, a mere distraction to be dismissed along the way to their morbid destination, a mosquito-like annoyance that, once gone, would leave these otherwise homogenous mourners to resume their solemn focus, to manage their private pain.

An icon had been brutally slain the week prior, one loved as viscerally as he was hated. Accordingly, the planned procession reflected the fallen's enormous stature as well as the important and troubling times in which he lived and died. Departing from Washington, D.C. on the morning of April 21, bedecked with black-fringed American flags and a portrait of the deceased, the casket-bearing train chugged northward on its 13-day mission, stopping for crowded memorial services in Baltimore, Harrisburg, Philadelphia, New York City, and Albany before cutting westward toward Illinois. Throngs of flag-waving mourners lined the tracks on both sides most of the way, many braving chilly winds and rain in the dark of night.

In Cleveland, ten thousand downtrodden citizens filed past the casket in a driving rain after the grim cargo was removed from the train and placed in an outdoor pavilion at Monument Square specially designed to accommodate the unprecedented crowd. A similar crowd showed up in Columbus the next day to watch as the coffin was carried in a 17-foot-long hearse to the State Capitol building before being assumed by eight members of the Veteran Guard, hoisted on to their broad shoulders, and carried into the rotunda.

Finally, in the early morning hours of May 2, 1865, the bruised and discolored body of Abraham Lincoln returned home as the much traveled railcar crossed the northwestern border of Indiana just south of Lake Michigan, into Illinois, a state to forever be associated with the fallen president's name.

Two days later, having been viewed by hundreds of thousands while lying in state at Chicago's Cook County Courthouse, and then again at the State House Hall of Representatives—the same State House that hosted his iconic "House Divided" speech seven years prior—the deceased was transported in a gold, silver, and crystal hearse on loan from the city of St. Louis past his Springfield home, past the Governor's Mansion, and onto the old country road leading to Oak Ridge Cemetery. The procession was led by Major General "Fighting Joe" Hooker, a controversial Civil War appointee of Lincoln known for his aversion to authority as much as his love of liquor and prostitutes. The hearse was followed by Old Bob, the slain leader's 16-year-old chestnut horse draped in a black mourning blanket.

The coffin was laid upon the marble slab inside a temporary receiving vault along with a second tiny coffin containing the remains of Willie, Lincoln's beloved son who'd succumbed to fever in the White House three years earlier. Lincoln associate and Methodist bishop, Matthew Simpson, gave the oration; family Presbyterian pastor, Dr. Phineas Densmore Gurley, read the benediction. The crowd watched solemnly as the vault's large iron gates closed and its heavy wooden doors thundered shut.

Not a moment too soon given the President's increasingly decaying exterior. Days earlier, prior to the State House viewing, the body's appearance had become increasingly distressed, a result of the passage of time as much as contrecoup, a phenomenon common to head wounds where the bullet causes contusions both at the site of impact and the opposite region as bones break and the brain slams into the skull. Lincoln's face, already considerably dark in life, covered this opposing point of impact, and with the resulting and severe bruising to the skin, darkened considerably more, an unacceptable development for funeral director, Charles Brown, and local undertaker, Thomas Lynch.

Offering a fix, Lynch slipped out of the chamber housing the casket, pushed through the determined crowd of viewers packing the corridors and stairways of the State House, and made his way to a neighborhood drugstore where he bought rouge chalk, amber, and a few brushes. Back at the State House, the resourceful undertaker took a half an hour to apply a thick coloring to mask the President's darkened features before thrusting open the chamber doors for public viewing.

Apparently color mattered much, even in death, a point that would not have been lost, had he been there, to the former passenger now sitting by the side of the tracks, head in hands, as unsure of his location as he was his purpose in life.

CHAPTER XXIII

SINS OF THE FATHER

Deep inside us, all of us, beneath years of conditioning and denial, lives an inescapable place where we know truth. It is a place of purity, existing despite our ongoing attempts to ignore or dismiss it, a site that winces when our words don't match our spirit, an inner location that, over time, with repeated infraction, soils then festers when we refuse to describe what we actually see. Though it is a place that can liberate us from our internal prison of self-hate and social conditioning, we choose instead to further imprison *it* and, in doing so, cement our own miserable fate. Such is our cursed existence, a humanity bound to hate what we love, fear what has birthed us, and imprison what would set us free.

All that remained was the mirror. Lincoln was gone, Spear was nowhere to be found, and a drunken, grief-stricken Paschal faced the fork-tongued glass with blood-soaked eyes, bottle in hand. What had once been a fearful respect for the flawless glass instrument had transformed into an intense hatred for the ancient object and its ambiguous riddles.

Still, since it was the only thing in his tumultuous life that had any permanence, the truth was, deep down Paschal still loved the mirror, though more like a child who recognized his own reflection in a present but unpredictable parent.

And here, at his lowest moment, Paschal thought of him, the one who had not been present.

Like the mirror, Pascal hated that he still loved him, and still hated him, despite the pain he'd caused, leaving him as a baby, abandoning him and his mother, relegating them to poverty to fend for themselves in the bowels of a violent and growing city, propelling him on his precarious, curious path in life. It was a path seeded long ago, back in a time when a virgin land, not yet Virginia, was new to some, but certainly not to those who'd been there as far back as anyone could remember. The Algonquian, the Iroquoians, the Siouan lived off the land wholly in tune with the natural maternal world sustaining them, one ripe with fertile soil, with lush, dense forests necklaced by hanging vines, waterways brimming with large, meaty sturgeon, scavenging crabs, and endless banks of oysters, and with clearings painted by colorful, wild, and delicate flowers consumed or trampled by varied stores of fowl, muscats, foxes, wolves, bears, and country lions.

Unfortunately for the natives, the animals walked on two feet as well, initially exploring then arriving over time, first on flyboats, then on *fluyts*, agile ships of Dutch origin primarily employed as mercantile carriers but commonly repurposed for war supply or expedited transatlantic travel. European settlement continued, particularly on behalf of the English Crown, failing often or barely succeeding, as was the case with the 1607 founding of the Jamestown colony. It was financed through its royal namesake's issuance of a charter to the London Company, a joint stock company that funded exploration and new settlements.

Such activity paved the way for subsequent settlements, and in the latter half of the century, for the introduction of the Cavaliers. The Cavaliers were those who had sided with the Crown in the English Civil War, had chosen to chance their aspirations in a new land without old politics and imposed restrictions to their wildest ambitions be they fiscal or proprietary, spiritual or religious, barbarous or carnal. Among them, the first American Randolph, William I, arrived in 1674 near current day Norfolk, initially appropriating almost 600 acres in Powhatan territory and labeling it "Turkey Island." He subsequently increased this to over 10,000 acres by any means necessary, including genocide and enslavement, on way to his ultimate status as a top tobacco producer, elected official, and one of the largest slaveholders of his generation by the time of his April 1711 death.

William's 1676 marriage to Mary Isham, an affluent widow rumored to be a descendant of Lady Godiva, produced ten children and scores of grandchildren and great-grandchildren who'd later establish and grow, by way of the blood, sweat, and tears of countless enslaved Africans, the massive Tuckahoe Plantation. Among their progeny were First Continental Congress president Peyton Randolph; Supreme Court Chief Justice John Marshall; president Thomas Jefferson; Virginia governors Edmund Jennings Randolph and Thomas Mann Randolph; and soldier and public official William Beverly Randolph, the latter being the absentee father of a brilliant, troubled adult now projecting his demons on the less than transparent glass surface staring back at him.

Still, the mirror was listening. Despite Paschal's stupor, it cast its spell upon him like the sweet, seductive words of a neglectful parent, pulling him into its womblike domain. It drew him beyond space and time, its flashing lights and spinning spheres pulling him deeper into its plasmic black vortex where, despite his previous trepidations, he would nonetheless listen as the mirror told the truth, even when it didn't, a riddled veracity, less than loyal, cloaked in sooth.

Be it the mirror, the alcohol, or a combination of the two, Paschal was floating weightlessly, suspended in aether, steadily moving toward infinity when the mirror spoke. This time it was a whisper, both through him and solely to him, in hushed, tantalizing tones, soft, warm, drenched in honey, bearing its ultimate third prophecy, one for all ages, announcing his path forward, only for Paschal to hear.

CHAPTER XXIV

THE MEETING

The spirit has ever been in the breath, the breath in the spirit. Its Latin root, *spir*, means "to breathe" as represented by such relevant and cyclical terms as *respiration, inspiration, expiration*, and *spiral*. Breathing, or respiration, is a two-phased process. The first is inspiration, where the lungs inhale, the diaphragm contracts and pulls downward as the muscles between the ribs contract and pull upward, expanding the thoracic cavity and enabling air to rush in and fill the lungs. The second is expiration, where the lungs exhale, the diaphragm relaxes, and the thoracic cavity contracts as air is forced out.

In the Land of the Nile, where breath was divine, the Opening of the Mouth was an important sacred practice, ostensibly designed to animate a nonliving entity, to breathe life into a formerly living being or its symbolic representative, and in doing so, transform the deceased into an akh, the enlightened, reanimated spirit. Consistently, the breath was sacred, divine, bearing life within its invisible presence, sustaining it in its spiraling ebb and flow. More than mere symbolism, this ancient process was accompanied by appropriate tools far too sophisticated to be deemed ceremonial, which they subsequently were, advanced instruments designed to aid artificial respiration and ensure the breath, the *spirit,* found its way back into the host, back into life, into being, into existence.

This animating process, passed down through the ages and colorfully enshrined on ancient walls, would inform both the practices of subsequent generations manifesting in the Bellows Method employed by Swiss physician Paracelsus in the 16th century where he inserted a fireplace bellows into the nose of those no longer breathing. Air generated through the bellows would be pumped into a victim's respiratory system to fill the lungs. However, the practice was largely undermined by the potential damage caused by the bellows itself, which was commonly filled with cinders, and by the harsh impact of such a mechanical blast of air on a victim's lungs

Centuries later, on December 3, 1732, at the mouth of a mine in Alloa, Scotland, surgeon William Tossach tended to a lifeless coal miner and produced what many at the time believed to be a miracle. Miner James Blair had suffocated and was carried 34 fathoms by two of his colleagues from the pit to the surface, reaching the doctor an estimated forty minutes after his last breath. In his 1744 self-recorded clinical account, Tossach recounted his dramatic experience twelve years earlier:

> *I made them immediately set him down at a little Distance from the Pit, turning him supine. The Colour of the Skin of his Body was natural, except where it was covered with Coal-dust; his Eyes were staring open, and his Mouth was gaping wide; his Skin was cold; there was not the least Pulse in either Heart or Arteries, and not the least Breathing could be observed: So that he was in all Appearance dead. I applied my Mouth close to his, and blowed my Breath as strong as I could, but having neglected to stop his Nostrils, all the Air came out at them; wherefore, taking hold of them with one Hand, and laying my other on his Breast at the left Pap, I blew again my Breath as strong as I could, raising his Chest fully with it, and immediately. I felt six or seven very quick Beats of the Heart; his Thorax continued to play, and the Pulse was felt soon after in the Arteries. I then opened a Vein in his Arm, which, after giving a small Jet sent out the Blood in Drops only, for a Quarter of an Hour, and then he bled freely. In the mean Time I caused him: to be pulled, pushed and rubbed, to assist the Motion of his Blood as much as I could, washed his Face and Temples*

with Water, and rubbed Sal volatile on his Nose and Lips. Though the Lungs continued to play, after I had first set them in Motion, yet, for more than half an Hour, it was only as a Pair of Bellows would have done, that is, he did not so much as groan, and his Eyes and Mouth remained both open. After about an Hour he began to, yawn, and to move his Eye-lids, Hands, and Feet…

Within four Hours he walked home…

Four decades after the resurrected Blair returned home, Danish veterinarian Peter Abildgaard experimented on a chicken and discovered that by shocking the heart through the chest he could restore a heartbeat. Then, in the 19th century, two methods dominated the medical landscape, the Hall and the Silvester methods. The Hall method involved the alternate repositioning of the victim from face up to the side, the Silverster method raising the victim's arms to expand the chest before crossing the arms over the chest and applying expiratory pressure. Less recognized yet more effective were the respective late 19th century innovations of two German scientists, Moritz Schiff and Friedrich Maass. Schiff restored the circulation in a dog undergoing open chest surgery after massaging its exposed heart in 1874. A decade and a half later, Maass successfully resuscitated two patients using external chest compressions, a process he ultimately coupled with respiratory ventilations, setting the stage for our modern approach to cardiopulmonary resuscitation.

However, decades before these German innovations, back during the height of the War between the States, a young Union officer effectively employed the Silvester method on the battlefield to save a fellow soldier who had ceased breathing.

Nearly three decades later, as a different kind of officer, this man would use a similar process to breathe life into another who had ceased breathing on the second floor of a Toledo apartment, a victim who claimed not to be a victim but a suspect, an old man prepared to issue his last breath, but not quite yet, given he had a story to tell.

And despite his precarious position, the cyclical flow of oxygen was just as sweet for him as it had been for those ancients reanimated long before him, the breath, ever divine.

———

"I knew him—or, at least, I somehow *felt* that I knew him and I had, of course, experienced his aforementioned demonstration in New York a decade prior. But others could not see beyond the subtle yet apparent African blood that covered his striking features, his abnormally large head, his deep set of intense, piercing eyes that, for a while, kept the whispered objections of uneasy passengers at bay until their collective cowardice conspired to form a critical mass and remove him from the procession of the man he knew far better than they. I watched those eyes carefully as they gazed past all of us as if in a lucid dream, or possibly an oft-practiced, non-confrontational trance to avoid the type of abrupt and disparate treatment he would subsequently endure. Once they removed him from the train, shunning his eloquent protests of medical title and presidential favor, I felt dirty, as if I were one of the red-faced, self-important rogues who had threatened him with slurs and ruffled his fine clothing while ejecting him and his belongings from the halted engine, an unplanned stop made just for him."

As if cued by disgust, the storyteller coughed violently, retrieving the white cotton handkerchief from an adjacent table and pressing it firmly to his mouth. Pulling it away, he impassively perused a smattering of crimson specks before reaching for a near-empty glass of water.

The uneasy detective shifted in his chair, wondering if he'd again have to save his self-proclaimed suspect.

Wiping his mouth, the old man returned the glass to the table and continued.

"There was something about him that drew me to him. Something different, almost otherworldly. I dare say a type of gravitational effect ... moon to Earth. Although I pride myself on my extensive vocabulary, I am at a loss to appropriately explain my feelings. But when I was in his orbit I could not pull away."

With a pensive pause, the storyteller's eyes darkened.

"Even so, there was something about this connection that *threatened* me. Despite his vulnerability, it was like he had this extraordinary power over me, like he held the very fate of my soul in his tiny hands."

The uncertain officer shifted in his seat, prompting his subject to snap from his trance and resume his story.

"Not long after Master Randolph's repulsive dismissal, I followed him from the train, a move that would ultimately lead me—and you as well, my good sir—here, to this room, on this eve, at the threshold of death's door."

The two men eyed each other in the middle of nowhere. Though not so far apart in age, their differences were apparent. One broad, white and impulsive, had been raised in a fairly well-to-do community in Connecticut with a stable family before setting out on his own as a soldier and journalist, eventually becoming a shorthand court reporter and special assistant for the War Department under Edwin Stanton. The other, slight, colored, brilliant, and conflicted both by his current disposition and the weightiness of his own identity, had been orphaned and reared in the slums, brothels, and streets of New York City, escaping to the high seas as a teen and traveling the world before pursuing his unprecedented and unusual life path.

They were different and yet the same. Both had a love of music and a passion for reading, travel, poetry, and the arts. Both were curious about the true nature of life, questioning the seen and the unseen. More immediately, both were miles away from the nearest train depot and had no idea what their next step would be.

They began walking and talking, and before long, it was as if no one else existed. The journalist posed many questions to the struggling man who'd compelled him to abandon the historic cross-country procession for the entombment of the country's fallen leader in favor of an impromptu roadside interview at the rim of a remote cornfield. By far it was the most compelling and unusual interview he had ever done. Paschal told of extraordinary events and times, of high seas and far off places, of rich cultures and exotic locales, of holding company with emperors and philosophers. With vivid detail, he described riding on camelback amidst the desert relics of Dongola; trekking on foot through the limestone mountains of Syria; scaling the Great Pyramid just before dawn to witness the heliacal rising of Orion from its hilt; basking in the therapeutic salts of the moonlit Mediterranean; swapping stories in fluent French with Dumas in a Parisian café; and hopping from country to country, across the globe, to study and compare the people, traditions, and cultures of each. The mesmerized storyteller clung to Paschal's every word as if his existence depended upon it.

He offered his thoughts on medicine and healing, on Spiritualism and its key figures and flaws, and on the costly war that had paved the way for emancipation while taking many lives, including the horrific postwar assassination of the friend that had brought them together. Though he would not elaborate on the full nature of his relationship with the controversial leader the country now mourned, Paschal did tell the spellbound journalist they had been introduced in 1851 by a mutual friend, had shared a special friendship, and how Lincoln had been an avid supporter of his aspiring but now jeopardized political career.

Referencing Lincoln, Paschal paused. His eyes watered and he located the late afternoon sun descending upon the western horizon. For the first time in four hours, silence enveloped the two men and they were forced to come to grips with the harshness of their current reality regarding both the fallen president and their immediate lack of bearing.

Finally, Paschal broke the silence and acknowledged the gravity of the moment by offering to recite a passage from the book he'd penned five years prior, *Dealings with the Dead*, examining the nature of death and the immortality of the soul. Closing his eyes, he spoke in an enchanted voice, the mesmerized journalist listening in awe.

"And we passed beyond the portal of the house, myself crossing at the same instant its threshold, and that of

Time; nor did I once cast a glance toward the frail and decaying shell from which a joyous thrill of super-consciousness told me that I had forever escaped; indeed I had no disposition to do so, for the reason that new and strange emotions and sensations crowded so fast upon me, that my whole attention was absorbed thereby; for they swept like the billows of a wind troubled lake, across the entire sea of my new-born being. One thought, arid one alone, connected with earth, assumed importance, and that was associated with the physical phenomenon of dissolution, and it shaped itself in a hundred ways with the rapidity of lightning — no, not lightning, but quicker, for that is very slow compared to the flashings and the rushings forth of thought, even in the earth-made brain; how much more rapid, then, from a source around which are no cerebral impediments to obstruct.

'Death — this is to be dead!' thought I. How blind, how deaf we are, not to see, and know, and hear, that all things tell of life, life, life — being, real and true; while nothing, nothing in the great domain of our God, speaks one word of absolute death, of a blotting out of Soul — Soul, which, while even cramped in coarse bodies, sometimes mounts the Capitals of existence, and with far-penetrating vision pierces the profoundest depths of space, gazes eagle-like upon the very sun of Glory, laughs death to scorn, and surveys the fields of two eternities — one behind, and one before it. This thing can never die, nor taste a single drop of bitter death!"

When a passerby offered his horse-drawn carriage to carry the unexpected tourists to the closest town that evening, the journalist felt like he'd known Paschal for an eternity and recognized that his own fate was somehow intimately tied to the plight of this peculiar man.

He also recognized this dark, extraordinary, grief-stricken man possessed the intellect and verse of a philosopher king and that, given the chance, Paschal would rule the minds of men.

CHAPTER XXV

PHILADELPHIA

*F*or *the first time since the death of Lincoln,* Paschal was back in his element. Philadelphia was abuzz with political energies as droves of Southern Loyalists descended upon the city five months after the passage of the Civil Rights Act of 1866 by a Republican-dominated Congress overriding the veto of President Andrew Johnson. The Loyalists, those southerners who had remained loyal to Lincoln's Union during the war, wished to rally their forces around an alternative plan of reconstructing the South given the violence and lack of effective federal protections many of them suffered from vengeful elements in the former Confederacy. Held the first week of September, mere weeks after the same city hosted the National Union Convention to marshal support for the president's agenda in the looming congressional elections, the Loyalists further pushed for the passage of a Constitutional Amendment granting citizenship rights to the formerly enslaved while heavily condemning Johnson for his Confederate-sympathizing policies.

Spear was back as well. Months prior, in anticipation of Paschal's invitation to speak at the Philadelphia convention, the military veteran had tracked him down in an effort to seize the moment and further grow Paschal's national political reputation. Though he had not heard from the colonel since the assassination, Paschal didn't question where the mysterious military man had been, particularly since Spear had come bearing gifts in the form of a brokered summer meeting between Paschal and Johnson at the White House where the President, in an attempt to pilfer a prominent Black figure from the Republican side, acknowledged his ongoing educational efforts with the Freedmen's Bureau in Louisiana and even pledged $200 to support it. After the meeting, a printed subscription of the popular spiritual journal, the *Banner of Light*, carried Johnson's recorded tribute to Paschal as "a man, an educator of his people, a true philanthropist, and a gentleman of very rare and unusual attainments as a scholar and orator."

Looking to grow that momentum, Paschal stood out like a colorful buoy amidst the wave of whiteness consuming Philadelphia's National Hall. His darker hue attracted curious looks, acknowledging smiles, or hostile stares largely consistent with the political sub-affiliations of the brim-bearing Loyalists. There were those who enthusiastically rallied for full emancipation, citizenship, and the franchise for formerly enslaved Africans; those who felt a more cautious, politically measured approach to the status of the Negro was appropriate; and a sizable faction mostly indifferent or outright hostile to the formerly enslaved given they simply wanted the retributive postwar attacks on their own southern lands, properties, and persons to stop. Either way, Paschal was well accustomed to reading such nonverbal communications, be they friendly, inhospitable, or somewhere in between. He nonetheless recognized this potential platform for resurrecting his aspiring political career since some of the pale faces now regarding him curiously could end up supporting his dreams.

Given the scale and politics of the conference, the media opposition was in full attack mode regarding the unfolding events in the "City of Brotherly Love." Along with vilification by local press, in a series of blistering headlines between September 2 and September 4, 1866, the *New York Herald* led the charge by pouncing on the mostly white men and handful of Negros and white women in attendance, characterizing the gathering as the Philadelphia "Mongrel Convention" and the "First Grand National Convention of Nigger Worshippers." If that wasn't bad enough, the *Richmond Times* referred to the gathering as a "Convention of Revolutionary Yahoos and Gorillas."

Such racial antagonism was by no means limited to the press or the opposition. Before leaving Louisiana to attend the convention,

Paschal had been elected a delegate. However, when he entered the hall, the convention now refused to recognize him because of his skin color, barring him from his delegate seat. After a heated exchange of words, a seething Paschal ultimately agreed to access the gathering as an unofficial member after promises that he'd later be allowed to address the convention.

Nationally renowned abolitionist, Frederick Douglass, was also in attendance despite being encouraged by a significant number of Loyalists, and threatened by some, to stay home and not attend the convention over concerns his presence would present a national distraction and cost them the support of several northern constituencies not willing to endorse the franchise for the formerly enslaved. Undeterred, Douglass not only attended the convention but subsequently recorded in his biography that he told those who encouraged him not to they "might as well ask me to put a loaded pistol to my head and blow my brains out, as to ask me to keep out of this convention." In an opening grand procession that featured over one thousand Union League members, four hundred convention delegates, and hundreds of Union veterans marching to music, fire-engine bells, and waving banners, the fearless Douglass entered Independence Hall marching arm-in-arm with white member Theodore Tilton, an influential newspaper editor, writer, and abolitionist, as a bold show of unity for the Black vote.

But if Douglass stole the show up front, it was Paschal who did so at its conclusion. On the 5th and final day—one day after a majority of the delegates from the Upper South and Border States walked out of the convention over their opposition to the promotion of the Black vote—a determined Paschal took to the stage to do what he did better than anyone else: *speak*. With the departure of the primary opponents to the Black vote, he recognized a more sympathetic audience and took full advantage of the moment to set the stage by speaking beyond their divisions to paint a compelling picture of what all had just endured, the costly war, the assassination of a leader, and the challenging aftermath. Caressing the audience with his words, Paschal peered into the eyes of as many audience members as possible to connect with their common humanity, to reach into their souls and appeal to their inner sense of morality, to instill in them that freedom and the full expression of such freedom meant just as much, if not more, to the formerly enslaved as it did to them. Once he had them exactly where he wanted, the talented orator, emphasizing key points via perfectly timed hand gestures and bodily movements, launched into an impassioned appeal that depicted the horrors of racial atrocity and clarified the need for reparation while demanding the franchise for all.

The mesmerized onlookers, many of whom who had heard curious rumors of the eloquent mulatto but had never seen him speak in person, hung on Paschal's every word, mouths open like infants anticipating the nipple. And just when they thought the moment couldn't get any bigger, it did. Amidst gasps, Paschal leapt from the stage to a heightened platform nearby and turned to acknowledge a massive portrait of Abraham Lincoln adorning the wall behind him before turning back to the spellbound audience.

I am not P.B. Randolph, I am the voice of God, crying, Hold! Hold! to the nation in its mad career! The lips of the struggling millions disfranchised demanding justice in the name of Truth—a Peter the Hermit, preaching a new crusade against Wrong—the Genius of progress appealing for schools, a pleader for the people, a toiler for the millions yet unborn, mechanic for the redemption of the world...

Dramatically flinging his left arm skyward in the direction of Lincoln's giant image, the animated orator shouted his final words. *"We are coming, Father Abraham!"*

A clear majority of the crowd exploded to its feet, clapping and shouting in approval. Douglass, who had spoken earlier and was seated up front next to Spear and noted women's rights advocate, Anna Dickinson, instinctively grabbed her Derby from her head and catapulted it into the air. In response, Dickinson seized Douglass' beaver shawl and whirled it about her head like a helicopter as Spear chuckled his approval.

Paschal breathed it all in while smiling broadly at the sea of animated white faces now beaming back at him. Five days prior, they had stripped him of his delegate status. Now they celebrated him as a hero for their common cause.

Or, better yet, a *king*.

The press in attendance had recorded his every word and Paschal well knew that in the days to come papers across the country, particularly the ones sympathetic to the abolitionist cause, would publish his address and depict the visceral impact it had upon the convention. He also knew the resulting momentum would make a viable platform for his reentry into the political realm, this time as a potential candidate for office in a reconstructed Louisiana with the desired political alignment of white Lincoln sympathizers and new Black voters.

For Paschal, who had endured daily discrimination from those far less intelligent than him alongside the painful loss of the powerful friend whose image loomed behind him, this was undoubtedly one of his finest moments.

From the back of the hall, the young journalist—the one he'd met a year prior after unceremoniously being expelled from the Lincoln funerary train—looked on with fascination, head cocked to the side, carefully studying the reaction of those in attendance. His eyes reclaimed the stage to take in the small, powerful speaker still basking in the crowd's relentless adulation before narrowing to slits, as if seeing something in Paschal that no one else saw.

Something potent.

Packing his pen and pad, he slipped out the side door of the hall.

CHAPTER XXVI

THE CARNIVAL KING

The party was one for the ages. New Orleans' most prominent and wealthy citizens were all in attendance, both white and Creole, dancing, drinking, and laughing on both levels of 1140 Royal Street. The two story mansion was a palatial structure adorned with intricate carvings, wrought iron balustrades, and massive chandeliers. Large golden trays bearing artisan-crafted delectables from the best French chefs in the region swarmed the masked revelers as the finest sparkling wine, exclusively imported from the newly-established Bollinger Champagne house in France, flowed freely as a mountain stream.

All eyes were on Paschal, who greeted a steady stream of anxious lauders, his colorfully beaded crown bearing the title "Carnival King" dangling off-center. As he turned to receive the moist, fleshy hand of the red-faced man with his other massive paw on Paschal's squirming back, a masked servant quickly stepped in to offer the overwhelmed celebrity a tray with a single flute of sparkling champagne at its center. Grateful for the diversion, Paschal received the glass, sipped, and nodded at the sophisticated attendant as the inebriated gorilla stumbled off toward the dessert table. Through his mask, the dutiful waiter winked back knowingly before receding into the revelry.

Then came the girl. No more than seven years old, her large, frantic eyes screaming from a jet-black face, she burst into the main room from the kitchen, stumbling, bouncing off of inebriated merrymakers who barely noticed her amidst the raucous festivities.

She zig-zagged through animated bodies, her head repeatedly whipping back over her shoulder as if being pursued by the devil.

Maybe she was. Following her bulging eyes, Paschal quickly located the source of her horror. The masked woman hosting the event, Madame Delphine, emerged from the kitchen door with purpose before going still, head cocked toward the terrified girl like a canine poised to pounce upon a pesky rodent. Coiled around her left fist was what appeared to be a leathery black whip. Statuesque and imposing, the focused woman remained frozen, watching the scrambling girl intently as everything moved around her, the servers, the dancers, the politicians, the socialites, the criminals, the high-priced escorts, all of them oblivious to her laser focus on her struggling prey.

Except for Paschal. The stunned crown-bearer became acutely aware that he was the only one conscious of the unfolding scene, that it was solely his to see, for whatever reason, wholly his to witness. As if taking cue, the terrified youth suddenly swiveled her head and peered directly at Paschal, her eyes begging his help. Their eyes locked for an eternal moment before the girl finally turned and disappeared through the entrance of a side staircase.

Shaken, Paschal could not erase the image of the girl's horror-stricken face from his psyche. Rubbing his eyes to discard it like some mucosal remnant of sleep, Paschal shot a glance back toward the kitchen to gauge the location of the hunter. What he saw chilled him to the bone, as the powerfully built hostess now stared directly at him.

Then, thankfully, mercifully, she disappeared. Paschal released the breath he'd been holding since the frantic girl burst into the room and attempted to regain his composure.

He did not, upon realizing the unique style of mansion they inhabited commonly included a stairway from the back of the kitchen up to the second and third levels, including access to the roof. Tormented by the girl's image, Paschal quickly maneuvered his way through the partygoers to the kitchen where he flung the door open and was greeted by at least a dozen sets of bloodshot eyes surrounded by a range of sweaty copper-brown and jet-black faces. He froze as they glared at him, no, *through* him, as if he were their oppressor, the one enslaving them and their children, the one forcing them to cook their master's food for their master's events in sauna-like conditions with little air flowing in or out. Paschal's eyes succumbed to the weight of theirs, plummeting downward before recognizing, in horror, that most of these involuntary chefs were actually chained to the massive cast iron stoves they tended.

Repulsed by the spectacle, Paschal became nauseous and his head began to spin. Still, he persisted, stumbling through the heart of the kitchen and its unwilling laborers to locate the small doorway at its rear leading to a narrow staircase. The young girl likely needed him and he was going to keep looking until he found her.

Scanning the structure's second and third floors, a disoriented, profusely perspiring Paschal came up empty. The girl and the Madame were nowhere in sight, as if they had vanished into the silky black night coating the outside of the mansion's many handblown-glass windows.

Then came the scream, jolting, bloodcurdling. It emanated from outside the structure, somewhere amidst the night sky, somewhere high above. Stunned, Paschal instinctively looked toward the window before remembering the third-floor access to the roof. He sprinted to locate the braided rawhide rope dangling from the hallway ceiling, pulled it down, and quickly climbed the portable stairway it revealed. Bursting through its small wooden door and into the night sky, Paschal's eyes danced wildly about the roof's baluster-rimmed surface before settling upon the broad back of the gala's hostess near its edge, her head angled downward. In her left hand she still bore the whip, though it now dripped with what appeared to be blood.

Despite his boisterous entry to the roof, Paschal noted that Madame Delphine had not turned around. He set out to approach her, but before he could get halfway, his eyes blurred and the woman's image split into two, circumnavigating each other like orbiting moons. Once again, his belly became nauseous as his perspiration drenched his clothing to a point it sagged from his body like a Roman toga.

Finally, with much effort and labored breath, he reached her. The broad-shouldered woman maintained her posture, eyes narrow, jaw set, peering out toward the ground below, barely acknowledging his presence. Breathing heavily, Paschal was just about to demand where the young girl had gone when he followed the path of the woman's eyes away from the roof and down to the ground three stories below. There, broken and twisted, illuminated by the light of the nearby party, lay the girl.

Paschal grabbed both sides of his head and shrieked in agony out into the night sky, as far as his voice, his pain, would travel. He had failed her. She had appealed to him to come and save her, and he had failed her.

Paschal glared at Madame Delphine's stoic face. From his side view, he watched in horror as a smirk slowly slid across her jaw. The woman was the devil.

"*Why would you do that?*" he demanded, head pounding, heart racing, tears filling the corners of his eyes. "*WHY???*"

Slowly, casually, the woman unlocked her gaze from her victim below and shifted it to Paschal. She looked *through* him. And then—first, almost inaudibly, then progressively louder—she laughed. Her laughter rapidly escalated into a full belly laugh, jarring, robust, maniacal.

Outraged, Paschal could take it no more. He lunged at the demonic woman but she seamlessly countered him, clutching his throat with an iron grip and hoisting him skyward with one hand like some hard-won trophy. Choking, tugging at his attacker's hand, toes frantically searching for bearing, the small man locked eyes with the Madame and, at first, recognized nothing human in the black, soulless pupils that burned back.

Then the blackness gave way to a floating canvas, a barrage of nebulous, emerging shapes and forms that danced and swirled before beginning to appear familiar. The pain stopped and the breath returned as all his focus was now upon the curious image flashing back, the one identical to him, his own reflection, staring back, crown and all, alike, and somehow… *different.*

It was the crown. It no longer bore the "Carnival King"

moniker and appeared more authentic, like real gold. Then the face blurred, morphing into something different, and again, familiar. And once again, he was the ancient king placing his hand upon the trembling head of the condemned poet pleading for his innocence while bound to a cold-metal stockade block in a dark, subterranean chamber of the palace in the royal castle of the greatest kingdom in the land, long ago.

"Plus de champagne, monsieur?"

It was not the response the king had anticipated. Wholly confused by the strange tongue of the poet, the puzzled king stepped back and glanced over at his vizier, who shrugged.

"My young man, I will certainly grant you the opportunity to speak your final words," said the curious king, flanked by the grimacing guard holding the razor-sharp sickle sword. "But I must admit my lack of familiarity with the words you now speak."

"Plus de champagne, monsieur?" repeated the poet, more urgent than the previous.

The bewildered king closed his eyes and it was Paschal who opened them, crown with "Carnival King" insignia back in place. Madame Delphine now stood before him, arms crossed, studying him with a triumphant, diabolical smile. Paschal instinctively raised his hands to protect his throat before recognizing the dutiful masked attendant who had served him earlier stood nearby with perfect posture as if nothing else mattered, eyes planted forward past Paschal, past the unhinged hostess, the dead girl three stories below, the endless night sky. In his right hand he carried a tray draped in black and topped by a single glass of champagne.

"Huh?"

This time in English. "More champagne, sir?"

Paschal's eyes blurred, his voice sputtering with incredulity. *"What*? What are you talking about? There's a *dead girl* down there who was pushed off of the roof by this sick—"

He was jolted by the sudden swivel of the masked waiter's head in his direction, his eyes burning into Paschal's skull. "How *dare* your highness show such mercy for the deceased?" scoffed the attendant, shedding the mask to reveal the face of the poet.

"Have you no shame? Where was your mercy for *me*?"

Stunned, Paschal stumbled back toward the roof's edge, unable to speak.

"I *loved* your daughter!" the poet shouted, closing in on the trembling man. "I would have honored her like no other, honored you, and honored your kingdom with my endless devotion. I would have been the *perfect* mate for her, the perfect son to you."

In one sudden and sweeping move, the red-eyed poet flung the tray with glass off the roof into the darkness to reveal the shimmering brass sickle sword the drape had concealed.

Paschal's heart leapt from his chest. He stammered his apology. "I-I am so, *so sorry*. I n-never wanted to—"

As Madame Delphine shrieked with delight, the young poet sliced Paschal's head from his shoulders, his crowned crown tumbling into the darkness below.

CHAPTER XXVII

AWAY

"*Master Randolph's dreams were perhaps as legendary as his intellect.*" The wide-eyed storyteller was hypnotized by the candle's steady flame. "I began spending more time with him to learn more of his esoteric teachings and he would, on occasion, share his dreams and visions with me. They were extraordinarily vivid, and as he relayed them, you almost felt as if you were a participant in them, somehow taking part in a parallel universe where Master Randolph dominated and all things revolved around him, be they nefarious or benevolent."

The old man paused, slightly narrowing his eyes at the stoic detective as if expecting his words to have a visible impact. Receiving no reaction, he continued.

"Despite his rigorous touring schedule as a popular national speaker, Master Randolph always made time for me and our lengthy and exhilarating discussions on life, on love, on loss, on nature, on physics, on creation, on matters of the spirit, the cosmos, the ether. We deconstructed Darwin, analyzed the electoral plight of the formerly enslaved, debated the challenging plight of the nation and the best path forward. We even traded our favorite passages from Longfellow and Thoreau."

To the detective's surprise, the infirmed man suddenly gathered himself and rose from his deathbed to a standing position far more capably than the stunned officer thought possible. His newfound agility was accompanied by an almost youthful expression. His face was less gaunt, his brows less bent as if suddenly energized by a great notion, one promptly rejuvenating him, reclaiming his long-lost youth.

Then he was Thoreau.

Away! away! away! away!
Ye have not kept your secret well,
I will abide that other day,
Those other lands ye tell.

Has time no leisure left for these,
The acts that ye rehearse?
Is not eternity a lease
For better deeds than verse?

'Tis sweet to hear of heroes dead,
To know them still alive,
But sweeter if we earn their bread,
And in us they survive.

Our life should feed the springs of fame
With a perennial wave,
As ocean feeds the babbling founts
Which find it in their grave.

Ye skies drop gently round my breast,
And be my corselet blue,
Ye earth receive my lance in rest,
My faithful charger you;

Ye stars my spear-heads in the sky,
My arrow-tips ye are;
I see the routed foemen fly,
My bright spears fixed are.

Give me an angel for a foe,
Fix now the place and time,
And straight to meet him I will go
Above the starry chime.

And with our clashing bucklers' clang
The heavenly spears shall ring,

While bright the northern lights shall hang
Beside our tourneying.

And if she lose her champion true,
Tell Heaven not despair,
For I will be her champion new,
Her fame I will repair.

Half smiling, the fascinated detective acknowledged the story-teller's inspired performance. "Away! away! away! away! Hadn't heard that one in years. My dad used to force-feed me Thoreau when I was young… have to admit such inspired words have grown on me."

The old man, once again looking every bit his age and health status, collapsed back to his deathbed in a heap of bones. "Yes, my dear sir," he gasped, with a wry smile. "Poetry is best served like a fine wine, properly aged over time."

The detective nodded his acknowledgment. "Sounds like the two of you had a wonderful relationship."

The old man maintained his gaze on the steady blue flame. "In many ways we did."

The officer shifted gears and demeanor. "Then why would you expect me to believe that you were responsible for his death? I mean, that's why you brought me here, right? This is supposed to be your grand confession?"

The question lingered, the storyteller maintained his gaze. After a long pause, he resumed.

"I pray you'll forgive me, my good sir, for taking this much of your precious time, but that said, you still won't grasp the gravity of the situation at hand regarding the untimely death of Master Randolph until you understand the full trajectory of the tragic account I am here to tell. So please, I beg you, bear with me, for by the time I finish, all will be clear. *Trust* me."

The detective settled back in his chair. The old man continued.

"With Spear at his side, Master Randolph's popularity soared as he toured the nation lecturing on a variety of relevant topics ranging from civil rights to temperance to sexual liberation to spirituality, also stumping for the Radical Republicans, the congressional constituency he'd closely worked with on the 1866 Civil Rights Bill. Because of his extraordinary intellect and charismatic storytelling, he mesmerized crowds, gaining hordes of supporters and attention wherever he traveled. His ongoing work and leadership in the New Orleans schools educating the formerly enslaved was celebrated across the nation by former abolitionists and related sympathizers, so much so that the unsympathetic president, Andrew Johnson, invited him to the White House in an effort to recruit him as a political ally.

But even with this increasing national political viability, Master Randolph longed to correct the grievous wrong committed upon him a year prior and pay proper homage to an old friend."

———

Seldom did a day pass when Paschal did not think about his late friend. Though tinged by melancholy, his recollections were useful as they invoked Lincoln's remaining spirit and provided him some form of solace, bittersweet yet comforting. In late 1866, amidst a growing backlash to the gains of Reconstruction, Paschal, along with Spear and the Radical Republicans, helped organize what came to be known as a Political Pilgrimage to the Tomb of Lincoln, a monthlong effort to rally around the political legacy and direction of the late president and, more personally, provide Paschal the closure he was denied when ejected from the funeral train a year prior.

Not only did Paschal actually make it to the Springfield, Illinois tomb this time around, for much of the trip, the spotlight was on him. Starting in New York City, each whistle stop in between hosted well-attended rallies and parades to further energize the political agenda of the Radical Republicans and each city included a roster of prominent speakers which those in attendance commonly viewed as oratorical contests, with one competitor ultimately winning the day. This being Paschal's wheelhouse, the results were epic, as many in the press hailed the aspiring political force for his superior oratorical prowess, often comparing him to his famed

146

associate, Frederick Douglass. Labeling him the "little Octaroon," the *Chicago Tribune* and other major papers of the day lauded his verbal gifts, noting how he excelled Douglass in *"description, word-painting, language, apostrophe, appeal, denunciation,—terrible, swift, merciless, and crushing,—and, withal, is an actor of such rare power that scene depicted becomes real to the audience. Nothing can excel his 'Prairie on Fire,' his 'Clink, Clink' scene; 'the Cobra Copello' adventure; 'Democrat in Heaven;' 'Descent into Maelstrom;' 'Pat and the Octoroon;' and the inimitable 'Bar Fite' away down south in Dixie, at the recital of which people are wont to laugh themselves sore from rib to heel, for his action is ridiculously absurd, while his talk is irresistibly funny."*

Despite his unmatched oratorical skill and soaring political star, what was *not* funny was Paschal's endurance of the daily racial slights and antagonisms that accompanied his hue even from those who praised him in public. At the Syracuse stop, event organizers had intentionally arranged for him to deliver his address alone on a platform during a rainstorm. In Missouri, the chairman of the pilgrimage, R. H. Branscomb, accused Paschal of stealing funds from event coffers and temporarily had him removed from the pilgrimage—kicked off the train once more—before reluctantly reinstating him upon Paschal's subsequent appeal to the residing governor of Illinois, Richard Oglesby.

Still, Paschal's light shone brightly and Spear knew it. As the train approached the Missouri-Illinois border, the colonel, sitting across from Paschal and squaring his broad shoulders, went into full military planning mode.

"Louisiana is obviously ripe for the picking. It's still a mess right now, but once our allies sort things out and take control of the political apparatus down there—which will happen soon—they will draft a new constitution and register new voters, including our formerly enslaved brethren who will receive the full rights due every citizen. Because of the Negro majority in this state, when this occurs, our opportunity to rally our substantial forces around you, both public and private, will be optimal. The timing could not be better," Spear acknowledged, a twinkle in his deep blue eyes.

Excited, Paschal smiled back, prompting additional military metaphors from the colonel.

"The enemy is flailing. We should launch our electoral attack directly at their core. Time to storm the castle and raise our flag. If you will allow me," continued the colonel, "I would like to start raising exploratory funds from our more heavy-handed friends and brethren both domestic and international to launch an exploratory committee for your potential Senate run in Louisiana. I sincerely believe that few would deny the opportune nature of the particular moment in which we find ourselves right now. It's time, my friend. It is time."

Paschal's heart leapt at Spear's confirmation of his rapidly increasing political viability, his apparent qualifications for such an opportunity. Finally, it all made sense. All that he'd endured to get to this current moment, the many years of tireless organizing, the countless rallies and stump speeches for other candidates or causes, the relentless racial slights and hostilities, his strategic and timely relocation to Louisiana, the earthshaking loss of his dear and powerful friend, the self-doubt, the fear, the ancient curse.

Paschal's time had come. And though Lincoln was no longer there to share it with him, he knew his old friend would be smiling from the realm of the spirits, from beyond the veil.

A grave look consumed the colonel's leathery, whiskered face. He spoke in a measured, deliberate fashion. "That said, the stakes are high, as the recent and tragic events occurring in New Orleans have made ever clear, the task at hand will be far from easy. There will certainly be those willing to do anything, to go to any length, to spare no expense to see it fail. To see *you* fail, Paschal."

Acknowledging the gravity of the colonel's sobering words, Paschal, thousands of miles away from the unique and troubled southern city he now called home, turned to gaze solemnly out the window at the beautiful countryside passing by.

CHAPTER XXVIII

THE SLAUGHTER

The slaughter was upon them. They had begun the day determined, despite dire warnings and serious threats of violence, to state their case. One rooted in the abduction, wholesale trafficking, dehumanizing, torture, confinement, rape, starvation, murder, decimation, degradation, miseducation, separation, isolation, and disempowerment of a people. They fully deserved and expected, *especially* given the extreme price they had paid, the full right to vote as citizens, to be counted in an electoral process that, for many years prior, had deemed them less than human.

As the parade wound its way toward the Mechanics Institute, the Greek Revival-style structure overlooking Canal Street and hosting the Louisiana Constitutional Convention, the hot July sun roasted their dark facades, this bold collection of freedmen, Union Army veterans, and convention supporters including women and children. Though they cherished life and the lives of their family members, they knew their silence was death and that their lives would not get any better if they did not take to the streets to show their solidarity with a convention orchestrated to bring about such change. They wanted equity, therefore, the Black Codes had to go, as they denied them the rights of citizenship and legally maintained their alleged inferiority, the false socioeconomic construct that had encouraged then justified their enslavement.

With a band leading the way, and hundreds of small American flags flapping from Black hands, the procession marched past a wave of rabid detractors composed of Confederate veterans, southern sympathizers, and local police as its front lines began entering the building.

Then all hell broke loose.

Outside the institute, a shot was fired. Then a second.

Weapons instantly appeared in white hands, distributed by the local police force prior to the parade, as the sea of pale-faced, bloodthirsty brutes descended upon the unarmed marchers, shooting, stabbing, and torturing those outside the institute before pursuing those fleeing for shelter inside to corner them and end their lives in pools of blood.

Led by police, the white savages set the building on fire. Those attempting to escape through windows were shot, tortured, beaten to death, or arrested.

By the time the bloodletting ceased, hundreds were dead and hundreds more wounded. The next day, with martial law declared by federal troops, the local press mostly downplayed the savagery, blaming it on "radical" actors looking to topple the social norms of the day. However, *Harper's Weekly* ran images nationally depicting armed white men gunning down Negroes fleeing the site. In his August 2, 1866 letter to General Grant, Major General P.H. Sheridan of the Union army, stationed in New Orleans at the time of the massacre, blamed the day's atrocities on the city's mayor, James T. Monroe.

"The more information I obtain of the affair of the 30th, in this city, the more revolting it becomes," wrote Sheridan. He clarified the event "was no riot; it was an absolute massacre by the police. It was a murder which the Mayor and police of the city perpetrated without the shadow of a necessity; furthermore, I believe it was premeditated, and every indication points to this."

———

As the train approached Chicago, Paschal reflected on the friends and associates he'd lost in the New Orleans massacre. If not for his recent travel north for the planning of the pilgrimage to Lincoln's tomb, he would have certainly been at the convention that day and likely dead, maimed, or incarcerated as a result. Instead, he was alive and on the final leg of a month-long journey that had its share of challenges, but nonetheless had greatly increased his political stock on a national level.

Paschal recognized his life had been spared as a matter of circumstance. But since he was not a believer in mere circumstance, he further recognized that everything happened for a reason, and that his life had been spared for a purpose. His time on Earth had additional meaning, and there was still a valuable role for him to play. Perhaps, he mused, the train he rode, both literally and figuratively, would take him to new heights in his political career, to cherished positions of leadership previously unimagined for those of his hue. Perhaps, as his mildly snoring associate, Spear, had acknowledged, his day had truly come. Perhaps the planets had aligned and Paschal was in full sync with his Earthly purpose, one propelling him forward and into a realm of power reserved only for the elite, those great few men who ruled the Earth, both through public and private channels, and forged history itself from their own skewed yet inspired vantage points.

Or maybe, as he'd feared, his accursed fate had been predetermined in a Promethean tragedy repeating since time immemorial, hounding him, keeping him alive just long enough for the dark, ancient energies to align, for reciprocity to complete its relentless juridical cycle.

Either way, Paschal figured he was alive and poised to make his mark upon history, not unlike the late friend he now traveled to commemorate.

Before Springfield, however, there was Chicago. With the accusations of theft leveled at him by the chairman of the pilgrimage, Paschal intended to deliver an oratorical performance that would dispel any notions of his alleged unworthiness to be the featured attraction of the pilgrimage. Spear backed this strategy and, as the two men gathered their bags and headed out the station, Paschal felt energized by the task at hand and comforted by the recognition that no one could command a podium as brilliantly as he.

CHAPTER XXIX

THE DESCENT

*T*he new politics writer for Harper's Weekly was well-connected.

A former war reporter, the Connecticut-born journalist had once covered New York's nascent spiritualist movement in the 1850s before recording the initial battles of the great conflict as a writer, then became a shorthand court reporter and special assistant for the War Department under Edwin Stanton. While working under the powerful Stanton, the journalist forged lasting and powerful connections in a variety of public and industrial sectors including manufacturing, railroads, petroleum, real estate, politics, the arts and, of course, media.

Only a few of these connections were a result of his government position. After following an enigmatic Black mystic expelled from the Lincoln funerary train a year and a half prior, the journalist followed that same man, who initially mentored him, into an elite society of powerful brethren who greatly expanded both his knowledge base and network.

Combined with *Harper's* national reach and status as the most read periodical in the country, the journalist was well-positioned to significantly influence culture and draw attention to issues or individuals he thought relevant.

With the high profile of the pilgrimage to Lincoln's tomb, and his relationship with one of its primary organizers, the journalist's first story proposal to *Harper's* editorial staff was a no-brainer. Plus, through his national political contacts, he'd heard rumors of an alleged scandal that had taken place during the pilgrimage that somehow involved his former mentor.

Chicago was a win. Not only did Paschal rise to the occasion as he had with his oratory so many times before, he'd delivered what many considered his finest performance in recent memory, easily trumping the other speakers foolish enough to share a platform with him.

As he descended the rostrum amidst the revelry shaking hands and greeting the sea of white faces he'd energized, Spear parted the crowd to slam a bear paw on the much smaller man's back. "Well done, Paschal! Well done!"

The imposing colonel then ushered him through the adulatory crowd and out onto Michigan Avenue, counseling him with an almost religious fervor as they made their way to their lunch date at the Michigan Avenue Hotel with a number of wealthy men and society brethren interested in backing Paschal's potential run for Senate.

"The fish are biting, Paschal." Spear was sweating profusely despite the cool fall air. "Time to reel 'em in. We play our cards right, and the state of Louisiana will never be the same. One of the first steps in that process is to go into this room with some of the richest men in the country and inspire them the way you just did on that platform. Let them know that with their backing, not only will we collectively change the direction of the country, but we will change the complexion of Congress, and perhaps one day with a healthy alliance between the Republicans and the formerly enslaved, the executive mansion itself."

Arriving at the hotel entrance, the inspired colonel stopped abruptly to look directly at the beaming Paschal. "I don't even know if our good friend Abraham would have seen that one coming."

As was common practice, Spear entered the establishment while Paschal remained out front so the colonel could ensure, either by persuasion or, if that failed, an outright bribe, that his exceptional Negro friend would not experience any hassles accessing the facilities. While he waited, Paschal pondered the colonel's encouraging words and imagined himself sitting, as Lincoln once did, behind the White House desk, signing off on the laws of the land.

His daydream was quickly interrupted.

"Good speech, Paschal."

The voice was familiar; the tone was not. It was like returning to a former childhood home to view its glossy new paint. He turned to see his mentee, the one who'd followed him from Lincoln's funerary train a year prior, calmly staring back at him. Paschal couldn't quite place it, but there was something different in both the eyes and demeanor of his friend. The younger man no longer addressed him as "Master Randolph" as he had before.

"Ah! My dear friend and brother!" Paschal smiled. "To what do I attribute this unexpected visit?"

The journalist's shoulders and demeanor loosened, only slightly. "I'm actually here on business. I just started writing for *Harper's*. I'm covering the pilgrimage."

"*Wonderful!*" Paschal was intent on rekindling the warmth of their previous relationship. An interview in such a popular vehicle like *Harper's* would go a long way toward establishing him as a viable national political figure, especially one drafted by a friendly author. With his current momentum, winning the progressive media was the critical next step in achieving a national office. "That is music to my ears. We need more capable reporters like yourself telling the story about what's really going on out here."

The journalist stiffened, brow furrowed as if hearing an offensive joke. He offered no response.

Paschal quickly recalibrated. "Well I am sure you know what you are doing. If I can help in any way to further enlighten you on the matters at hand, please don't hesitate to ask."

"Indeed, I will Paschal. In fact, I'd like to interview you on the pilgrimage and its political significance for you going forward as soon as possible."

Paschal responded in his warmest voice. "Anything for you, my dear friend."

———

The charge was on. Spear was in great spirits, more animated than usual after the successful meeting with potential campaign supporters in Chicago the week prior. Paschal was in demand as a speaker across the country as political groups and supporters of universal suffrage reached out to secure him for their events or rallies. Laws were being challenged or changing in many states to extend the franchise to the formerly enslaved. And the *Harper's* piece was slated to run nationally within the coming days. Even though Paschal had been a bit thrown by his journalist friend asking questions about the alleged theft scandal, he was excited to be featured in the top paper in the country. It was an indicator of how far he'd come from barely surviving the unforgiving streets of New York as a confused and impoverished youth.

Unfortunately, when the national article was finally released days later, Paschal was devastated. Rather than focusing on his unlikely success or the promise of his burgeoning political career, the piece primarily concentrated on the alleged theft scandal and its more salacious and unproven aspects while providing a platform for his accusers. Branscomb, the chairman of the pilgrimage, trashed Paschal's reputation, labeling him both opportunistic and "untrustworthy." One of the chairman's colleagues painted a picture of how the "underhanded" Negro orator diabolically induced the committee leadership into believing in the purity of his political messaging while all along plotting to divorce the committee from its much-needed operating funds. A third source, someone he'd never met or even heard of before, claimed he'd actually witnessed Paschal at the scene of the crime with his "hand in the cookie jar" stealing funds from the small wooden box used to collect them.

Though such claims were wholly unsubstantiated, the damage was irreversible. Those who previously flocked to him to shake his hand, exchange pleasantries, or drink at the fount of his wisdom, now hovered at a distance pointing in his direction as if navigating a rabid dog from a secure location. His key supporters balked and fled, taking with them their sizable sums of money and influence, leaving Paschal with little capacity or leverage to launch a viable political campaign. Spear disappeared again, no explanation, no parting words.

Once again, his world had turned upside down. Paschal was utterly alone.

Two weeks after the release of the *Harper's* article, distraught, Paschal was back home in Louisiana with few options, political or otherwise, bottle in a hand, writing then soliloquizing on his cursed existence.

Every genius is ticketed for misery in this life; for theirs is but an angular, one-sided, painful development. A few advantages are purchased at an enormous cost. A short, brilliant, erratic career, more kicks than praises; more flattering leeches than fast friends; rich and joyous to-day, houseless and suffering the pangs of hell tomorrow; understood by God alone; seldom loved till dead; the victims of viciously minded men, and the solitary pillars of life.

Genius is a bright bauble, but a dangerous possession; invariably open to two worlds. They are assaulted, coaxed, flattered, led captive on all sides through their affectionate nature. Rest comes to them only with death; and peace comes only through the knowledge of having done their best. They are compelled to train all their previously neglected facilities to something like harmony with those few wherewith they startled the world. As an example: A man who is a great architect, musician, physiologist, painter, sculptor, poet, or reasoner, must cultivate all his other faculties until he becomes rounded out. He thus outgrows his special angularities, and develops into a different man altogether. As he does this, he is most apt to lose his genius and be no more than a common man.

It is a blessed thing to be able, as I am, to tell all such, and all the other tearful, unknown, sad-hearted, weary

Souls, the unpitied, unappreciated wives; the struggling, honest man who goes to the wall because he cannot pollute his Soul by chicanery and low knavery, whereby coarser men find thrift; I repeat, it is a joy to me this night to be able to pen these lines of assurance that in very truth there is rest, and peace, and sweet sleep, and comfort, and sympathy and appreciation; and there are warmly loving hearts waiting for them in the beyond; and how some of us will rest, when our year of jubilee shall come, and death sets us free.

CHAPTER XXX

A WALKING SHADOW

"*Well, my good sir, our time appears to be running short.*" The laboring storyteller peered into the bloody handkerchief he'd just used to cover a violent fit of coughing.

Though the seasoned detective was certainly no stranger to blood and knew the old man's expiration date had arrived, he nonetheless recoiled slightly at the sight of the stark red plasma on the white cloth.

Still, the verses continued to flow.

> *Tomorrow, and tomorrow, and tomorrow,*
> *Creeps in this petty pace from day to day,*
> *To the last syllable of recorded time;*
> *And all our yesterdays have lighted fools*
> *The way to dusty death. Out, out, brief candle!*
> *Life's but a walking shadow, a poor player,*
> *That struts and frets his hour upon the stage,*
> *And then is heard no more. It is a tale*
> *Told by an idiot, full of sound and fury,*
> *Signifying nothing.*

"Shakespeare, Macbeth," the detective issued confidently.

"Right again, my dear sir! Apparently, there is no riddle too great for you." The old man smiled.

Then he fell silent, his eyes dimmed, his demeanor shifted as if all the wind had been taken from his lungs. Eyes closed, the storyteller ceased speaking for a full five minutes. The attentive officer kept his eyes glued to the old man's chest, checking for its rise and fall.

Finally, the old man's eyes opened slowly and his silence gave way to regret.

"I am not in any way proud of what I have done," the storyteller lamented. "When Master Randolph was riding high, and perhaps at the pinnacle of his career, it was I who wielded the pen that delivered the death blow to his promising career. With his high-powered political connections, extraordinary intellect, and charismatic oratory, he could have easily won a Senate seat in Louisiana. And then, from there, who knows how high he could have risen, especially with his popularity among both Negroes and the Radical Republicans?"

The old man shook his head.

"The possibilities still boggle the mind. Yet I chose to destroy him and everything he stood for, the man who took me under his wing and counseled me, who introduced me to the true wonders and mysteries of the surreal world we live in. He showed me there is more, so much more beyond the veil, the thinly constructed illusion separating life from death and man from God. Indeed, Master Randolph showed me myself, the full being I really had been all along, although, to his detriment, he failed to recognize it himself."

"But who was I? Better yet, who *am* I?" begged the storyteller, in the general direction of the detective. He paused, his soiled lips quivering under blood-streaked eyes.

"Whatever I was proved wholly detrimental to Master Randolph. In fact, he wrote and warned of the likes of me, perhaps not specifically, but he certainly had me in mind when…"

The old man's eyes suddenly darted with renewed vigor to the bookcase. The detective complied. "Third shelf from the top, maroon spine, *Eulis: The History of Love*, Master Randolph. Yes that one. Thank you, my good sir. It was published shortly before his death, just prior to that tragic moment fifteen years ago that has brought us here today."

Clearing his parched throat, the feeble man slowly opened the worn text.

The rank and file of this trouble-making army wouldn't pass muster at the gates of Heaven; for a more ungenerous, malignant, back-biting set was never developed by any civilization Earth ever saw. Born of loveless parents, they rush through life striking alike, hap-hazard, at friend or foe; discontented from the nipple to eternity; full of malice; steeped to the lips with cruel, cool, cobra-like venom, they are never happy save when slandering their betters, picking flaws in others' characters, and in stabbing in the back those whom they dare not face. Beware of such! They abound, and like some snakes, not on legs...

I am a Sang Mélee; and not less than twelve strains of blood rush through my veins, yet have I ever met insult all the way along of life, because I dared to be myself! But triumphantly have I done that same thing, 'and all despite my good Lords Cardinal,' from the early days till now,—Selah! For the fault of the Infinite, if fault it was, to make me of an unfashionable cast, have I been almost crucified, and have suffered, as it were, a thousand deaths. For the Madagascan tinge on my cheek, not its volcanic fires in my soul—Fires which held the cowards at bay for five and thirty years—have I been doubly wronged, by these and them and those, who, when help was needed, gladly availed them of my brain and speech and pen, to devoutly damn me when the fights were won!

Driven by the flaming sword of mean prejudice from all noble occupation and employment, by those whose pallor, alone, not Soul, or Honor or Manhood, or nobility of character, made them strong, and gave them warrant to invade my rights, and darkly slander me,—and invariably behind my back! lacking manly courage to do it to my face,—cowards, all, whom I felt and feel were, and are, as far beneath me as the floor of space is below the loftiest Turret of the Immeasurable Temple wherein God resides! Attacked with bitter and envious malignity, ever without the chance of reply,—by tongue and pen,—still I survived; and—despite them all. Treated more like a beast of the jungle than a human being; they exhausted all logic trying to prove me a nobody,—themselves the only real thinkers; and in seeking to justify their own outrage, really vindicated me! They thought it better to denounce and slay me, than to afford me a fair, free field to contest in the matter of Mind!—heaping abuse and contumely on me all the while, yet what availed it all? I became a Power in the world! What are they? I took to Mirrorology, and they did not like it, because it enabled me to laugh their isms and practice to utter scorn!— just where and as, I hold them to and in this hour! But their hostilities—in all these years—drove me back upon God and my own soul; and I prefer being called all the names the discontented could or can apply, to being counted among their malign confraternity, because my Philosophy taught me to forbear retaliation, seeing they could not help doing as they did...

Oh, how I have yearned for everlasting death, in view of the pitiless, remorseless persecutions, insults, wrongs, heaped on my head by thousands whom I never either harmed or even met—envious, jealous, sordid! I pitied them, and longed for lasting rest. It is not so now, for the victory is mine, and I pity and forgive them all...

———————

"But I am still not understanding *why*," the perplexed officer pleaded, revealing his first sense of urgency. "If everything you say about this man is true, then you should have been praising him, not destroying him. You consistently refer to him as your friend and even your 'master' while exalting his intellect and charisma. You even recite his words as if they were your own, poetically pronouncing each syllable as if it were your last."

The old storyteller did not respond.

"So," the pressing detective continued, "I am going to ask the same question I asked before, the one you have yet to answer. Why do you feel that you are responsible for the death of a man that all evidence shows took his own life over fifteen years ago?"

CHAPTER XXXI

TOLEDO

*T*he strange man staggered about the cobblestone street launching obscenities at anyone who would listen, particularly the young woman he called his wife, the mother of his infant son, the one hiding out in the neighbor's house upon betraying him with another neighbor after he'd found her out.

Eyes blood red, speech slurred, the man knew, just like his promiscuous spouse, the world had wronged him yet again, had taken his vision of happiness along with his heart and dashed it on the rocks, a surging wave throwing a helpless ship against unforgiving cliffs and destroying what had been. Like many former mates, the young woman had been drawn to him for his superior intellect, his extraordinary verbal capacities, his breathtaking stories and experiences, and his exotic hue, a student worshipping an inspiring teacher and following him home after class. But over time, inspiration succumbed to the evils of proximity as reverence descended into tolerance, then annoyance, then animosity. The Negro was no longer magical; he was just another nigger.

Unfortunately for Paschal, marital infidelity was far from being the only motive behind his inebriated state. A day earlier, the colonel had paid Paschal a visit almost a decade after disappearing from the ill-fated pilgrimage to Lincoln's tomb. Once burly and impressive, Spear now appeared fragile, disheveled, with sunken eyes and the drawn face of a Basset Hound.

The bold, confident military leader was no more. Spear stood at Paschal's stoop, hands clasped, eyes downward, and spoke quietly, the timid tones of a voice betrayed by its own regretful past.

"Paschal, I—"

"What are *you* doing here?" Paschal was simultaneously stunned and annoyed. His eyes bounced about the former soldier attempting to quickly reconcile his celebrated past with his current disposition.

They could not.

"Please, Paschal, I beg you. I just wanted to—"

"*Disappear?*" Paschal snapped bitterly. "Isn't that what you do?"

Spear fell silent, eyes pinned to the ground. He recognized that any words he had to offer would not be heard, at least not until he endured the ones biting back at him.

"Wow! What a magic act!" chided Paschal. "I can see why you must have been an incredible soldier. You could disappear before the enemy could see you. Then again, you could also disappear in the heat of the battle whenever your men needed you most, right, Colonel?"

Spear shifted his feet as if there were a rock in his shoe. Finally, after a significant stretch with no words from either man, he spoke.

"Paschal, yes, I failed you in far more ways than one. That's what I am here to talk about. I have a confession to make. And I am sure once I say it out loud you will certainly despise me and my visit even more. But it has to be said, for my soul cannot rest if I continue to hold it in, and you have every right to know what actually happened on the pilgrimage a decade back."

With these unexpected words, Paschal's disposition immediately shifted from irate to curious.

"At the time of the journey to Lincoln's tomb, I was not well," Spear said, his eyes cast down, not making eye contact with Paschal. "Indeed, I was hooked on opium. Had used it for years to quell the pains of wounds sustained in battle. So in the state that I was, I did a lot of things that I still am not proud of. Some of these things caused great turmoil for other people, particularly those closest to me. And I don't know if I'll ever be able to live that down."

Spear's eyes rose cautiously to meet Paschal's. True to his weaponized name, the former military leader's words would pierce his former friend's heart.

"It was me, Paschal, back on the train to Chicago."

Brow raised, Paschal's hardened demeanor softened with vulnerability. "*What* are you saying? What about the train to Chicago?"

"It was me, Paschal. I was the one who stole the funds from the event committee coffers."

The threats were growing louder, more ominous. Paschal launched another stream of obscenities at his young wife from outside her place of hiding, the home owned by her sympathetic neighbor and parttime babysitter who believed her to be both too young and too white for her heavily intoxicated husband. Spear had betrayed him, and the woman he loved had done the same. Someone needed to pay.

To the horror of the two women peering out the window amidst the shrill cries of the agitated, bassinet-bound infant behind them, Paschal reached into the back of his pants, pulled out a Schofield six-shot revolver, and fired.

CHAPTER XXXII

MOURNING DOVE

"*C*oo-ah*, coo, coo… coo-ah, coo, coo, coo…*"

Zenaida macroura, the species more commonly known as mourning doves, are among the most popular birds in Ohio. The mourning dove is of a brownish hue with gray and pointed falcon-like wings and a long, tapered tail speckled with large white spots. The prolific bird is known to get the most out of its lengthy, aerodynamic appendages, flying at speeds of up to 55 mph.

Mourning doves, at least according to lore, are not only monogamous, they are often mates for life. Commonly seen enjoying each other's presence, cuddling lovingly, they are named for their characteristic melody, a low and mournful "*coo-ah, coo, coo, coo… coo-ah, coo, coo, coo.*"

This characteristic call proved to be the final verse of the rapidly rising dove, the aspiring and unwitting creature that, moments earlier, had taken flight from stockpiling seed off the ground below before being inadvertently shot from the sky by the distraught colored man mourning his broken relationship with the young and less than monogamous woman he'd believed to be his mate for life.

Once again, he was confronted by his own reflection. Dejected, Paschal sat alone in a small parlor of his single-story Toledo home facing the antique mirror. The dimly-lit room cast an eerie shadow about his reflection as if portraying a visual manifestation of the curse hounding him daily, plaguing his psyche, his relationships. And like the pristine glass projecting back at him, one thing was undeniably clear.

Aside from the mirror, Paschal was alone. Truth be told, since the early death of his mother, he always had been. In many ways, the mirror had raised him, even nurtured him. In doing so, it enabled some of his greatest gifts; at times, however, it had scolded him, struck him back down to Earth without warning like an envious parent. Both mother and father, the ostensibly transparent glass represented the former in its constant presence and unconditional love, the latter in its riddled motives and estrangement. It had buoyed his aspirations and manifested his dreams, dashed his hopes and obscured his vision. Still, it had never lied to him. Rather, the mirror had misled him with false truths, deceptive visions that played upon his hopes, his wants, his desperate longing, rooted in his stunted childhood, to be loved fully, maternally, despite his lifelong lack of affection for the distraught reflection staring back at him.

Then the image morphed, regressed, and he was young again. An anxious, wide-eyed five-year-old caged in a riverside bluestone structure clamoring for the ghost of his mother while cringing from the weight of an ancient curse; a terrified ten-year-old in a tiny bedroom shivering under the vindictive gaze of a bucket-yielding relative; a despised and brutalized teen at sea leaping to take his own life; a mystic in trance exploring other worlds, plagued by the racism infecting his own; an unofficial presidential advisor misreading a forked-tongue prophecy beneath the White House; an ancient king being beheaded by a young poet at his royal wedding; a formerly celebrated orator being targeted by New Orleans' white supremacists for his teachings and ostracized by the city's Black leaders for his arrogance; a reluctant witness reeling from a fireside self-sacrifice in Congo Square; a distraught Order leader learning of the assassination of his close friend and society brother; a rising politician felled by the treachery of a trusted associate; an inebriated, pistol-packing husband threatening his barely-adult wife of a different race in the middle of a Toledo street.

This time was different. Paschal's trances were consistently all-consuming. An extreme amount of energy was required to pull such imagery from the flawless glass and provide their vivid nature. Still, the images that played out before him felt more reflective than visionary, like a regretful elder reviewing a tragic and unfulfilled life journey. For Paschal, the realization was sobering, suggesting new possibilities and prompting him to rethink his relationship with his mirror and what he believed to be his cursed existence. Perhaps the mirror was a mere reflection of what he wanted or did not want to see. Maybe it was nothing more than a reflective tool, a finely crafted instrument incapable of *doing* anything to anyone other than simply displaying the energies projected on it, be they fearful or rose-colored, hellish or hopeful. And maybe he had the choice, the power, all along, to see his own life as a blessing or a curse rather than leaving it to the whims of some accursed prophetic instrument vested in his demise.

Paschal's reflective trance was broken by an unexpected knock at the door. Likely someone had informed the city MP on area patrol that a crazed, intoxicated colored man with a white wife was firing a pistol in the middle of the street. With little venom or energy left to dispute his assumed arrest, Paschal sighed heavily before heading toward the door and flinging it wide open.

The tiny parlor felt even smaller as the two men stared at each other silently, a bare light bulb flickering above, the mirror looking on. The formerly young journalist looked a lot less so, his coal-black eyes far from innocent, his face fuller, his demeanor seasoned by experience. He stood calmly, hat in hand, before Paschal, who was seated.

Finally, the newsman broke the silence. "After that hit piece I wrote on you in *Harper's*, I'm pretty sure I am the last person you want to see, Paschal."

"Oh, don't be so sure about that," Paschal replied glumly. "Between you, my wife, and the colonel, the competition has been pretty steep."

Not waiting for an explanation, the newsman continued. "I'm now an editor with the *Toledo Blade* here in the city and—"

"Wonderful." Paschal rolled his eyes.

"—and I wanted to stop by to tell you something that you should know. Something that I have dealt with for years. It's about your mirror, Paschal. I know it harbors secrets, and I've known this since the first time I experienced one of your demonstrations many moons ago, back in New York. In fact, your extraordinary presentation that day changed my life."

Intrigued, though still jaded, Paschal slightly raised a brow. "If I had a dime for every time an impressed audience member told me I changed their lives, I would be living in a villa on the French Riviera, not here in Toledo."

The visibly weary host turned to face his unexpected visitor. "So what is it that you want? What do you have to tell me that was so important that you left your *lofty* position as editor of the *Blade* to track me down at my humble abode?"

The journalist nodded in acknowledgement of Paschal's less than enthusiastic response. Then, to Paschal's surprise, the unexpected visitor, who had never been to his Toledo residence—a man Paschal had not seen for years and didn't even know that he shared the same city—glanced out to scan the hallway before closing the door to the small parlor.

"I can show you better than I can tell you."

He scanned the ceiling and tugged the dangling chain of the inverted bulb before stepping toward his slightly offended, though curious host in the dim setting. For an eternal moment, the man stared deep into Paschal's eyes, then nodded toward the mirror.

Sensing something different in the journalist's demeanor, Paschal complied, intrigued, and the two men gazed into the transparent glass that framed their mutual existence.

"*Coo-ah, coo, coo… coo-ah, coo, coo, coo…*"

Baby in tow, the young woman watched spellbound as the dove nudged its fallen mate, using the top of its head in a futile attempt to reanimate the bloody, deceased bird and make it fly. Despite the apparent tragedy, the mourning dove did not abandon its mate, a fitting demonstration as she now headed home to reclaim her own given her lack of life experience and necessary support for her wailing, needy infant.

Once there, she began wailing as well upon discovering the lifeless body of her husband with a single shot to the head from an adjacent pistol, his crumpled form fronting their antique mirror.

And with his demise came the fulfillment of the third and final prophecy, the riddled prediction whispered solely to Paschal by the sooth-bearing glass a decade prior that had, once again, presented a truth less than true, had assured the now deceased man with the thin stream of blood trickling from his head that *you will once again establish your bloodline upon the Crown.*

CHAPTER XXXIII

THE POETRY OF IT ALL

"*I have not been dishonest with you,* good sir, for deception is no longer my path. However, I have refrained from being *wholly honest.* Not to mislead you, but rather to set the stage for my guilt, which you would struggle to comprehend if I had not described the surrounding theater in such a painstaking way.

Our interests tragically aligned. Stanton wanted Lincoln dead in an effort to consolidate his own power through his presidential successor; I needed the president out of the way in order to thwart the increasing power of the Lincoln ally who cursed my existence long ago—truly a tragedy of Shakespearean proportion."

The old man paused, contemplating words yet spoken. Brow furrowed, the detective tilted his head to study the dying man's weathered face.

The storyteller coughed violently, a red spray escaping his lips before his frail handkerchief-bearing hand could gather the erupting crimson release. Caught off guard, the wide eyed detective jumped to his feet, knocking the chair to the floor. Once up, he remained in his spot, recognizing the futility of his action. Glancing down, he noticed red specks on his otherwise flawless black boots.

This time, the old man failed to acknowledge the detective's reaction, so wholly consumed was he by the gravity of the moment and the inadequacy of the soiled cloth he clutched to his mouth. He spoke slowly, his trademark eloquence less convincing.

"It is time for the final act, my good sir. The inevitable is upon us. I must complete my story."

The detective sighed, righted the chair, and reclaimed his seat. The candle flickered, its diminishing wax oozing to its ultimate demise.

His voice a near whisper, his eyes dying embers, the storyteller resumed.

"That enchanted evening in New York… that sublime, magical, accursed eve. Though it was the first time I'd ever encountered Master Randolph's presence in the physical, my soul had known him for eons. That night at the theater changed everything. I watched a man, a master of his craft, transform before my eyes into another being, another *soul,* and in doing so, reveal my own.

It would be hard for me to effectively describe the impact of Master Randolph, his mind-bending presentation, his antique mirror. Both man and instrument were wholly magnetic, as they would have been independent of one another. But their *combined* mystical power was overwhelming, irresistible, their interaction forming a vortex and generating a centripetal force that drew me to their sublime symbiosis, their enchanted duality.

That night, after the demonstration, my descent into the facility's underworld was transformative in ways that are nearly impossible to express. Reaching the bottom of the stairway, I somehow knew which direction to move despite the room's enveloping darkness."

His breath increasingly labored, the old man momentarily closed his eyes and gathered himself as if preparing for one final effort. He opened them again, his resolve clear.

"It was the mirror, calling me, seducing me, summoning me to its divine presence. I approached it slowly, and with each step, a dark, hazy image I thought to be my reflection began to emerge. But it wasn't—and yet it was. I was somehow younger, more vibrant, more determined...

You see, that night, the mirror *spoke* to me, melodically, sweetly, stripping me down to my bare essence, exposing me for the vengeful, thirsty, and insatiable soul that I was. That I *am*. Although I didn't put all of the pieces together that night, it set me on my journey of self-discovery... That mirror showed me the story of *me,* from whence I came. Far from a short story, to the contrary, one forged by the ages, perhaps as old as time itself. It was a story of love, of loss, of unconsummated romance, of stunning betrayal… of poetry."

The full moon bathed the cover of evening in an enchanted glow, casting an electric blue energy over the land, surreal in its demeanor, endless in its possibilities. Though over the course of the day the entourage had covered countless difficult miles of hard, open country, their magical surroundings urged the young poet onward as if bound by spell.

Finally, on the 33rd cycle of the sun, the weary band came upon the kingdom, the grandiose abode of the world's most powerful ruler. It was the legendary dwelling of his virgin daughter, the most beautiful princess in all the land.

The magic continued over the following months as the poet, when not fulfilling his interpreting duties between his embassy and the kingdom, frequented the grotto behind the palace, the quiet spot located unbeknownst to him under the balcony of the princess. There, he recited poetry, sang, and pondered the king's riddle, the one if answered correctly guaranteed him the princess' hand in marriage or, if not, his prompt execution. Still, though it was a time of curses, the poet harbored no fear for it was equally a time of miracles, a time of extraordinary events and fantastic feats of daring, of epic tales to be told and retold down through the ages, through song or verse, to live forever.

Sadly, the miracle that got him there could not sustain him as the diabolical Grand Vizier encouraged the gullible king to betray the young poet, executing him unjustifiably in an underground chamber in the dark of night. In doing so, he betrayed the laws of nature and doomed them all, down through the ages, to the ends of time, or at least until the cursed king could somehow shed his onerous hex and regain his kingdom.

The old man broke his reflective trance on the ancient saga that played out on the canvas of his mind. Eyes closed, he began repeating the last passage of the ancient kingdom curse from *Ravalette*, this time without the aid of the book.

> *'Twas a curse further empowered by the hasty midnight burial of the poet's remains beneath the balcony of the distraught princess where, every day, her endless tears would plummet earthward and, unbeknownst to her, water the bones of her vanished love, nurturing them and the curse they carried, by reason of which thou, O king! and thou, O vizier! and the dead man, have all changed the human for another nature, as all shall continue, down through the ages, reincarnating from form to form, eternally damned, in an endless saga, with the king, ever tempted by the conniving vizier, ever thwarted by the poet, ever aspiring to reclaim his full kingdom, power, and adoration.*

The detective watched in awe, hearing what he believed to be the delusional rantings of a dying man.

The storyteller's next words confirmed his suspicion.

"For *I* am the poet… the artist, the dreamer, the one who would give his life, who *did* give his life, for the pursuit of art, for the thrill of passion… for love. It was a love for the ages, one never consummated, and so it remains."

The room fell silent, the detective frozen by the abnormality of the moment. After an eternal pause, the old man opened his eyes and switched gears.

"I truly worshipped Master Randolph. He was a king among men. His unparalleled intellect, his extraordinary presence, his stunning clairvoyance. He was royal in so many ways."

Ashamed, the storyteller shook his silver head.

"The irony of it all… Although I have devoted lifetimes to preventing his kingship, I have a dying need to inform others of the king once living among them… and yet I have *hated* him with all of my being. I have cursed him, tracked him through the cycles of time to ensure he never reclaims his throne, never regains his precious kingdom.

Fifteen years ago, on his final day, it was I who visited him and showed him once and for all—at least in *this* lifetime—my true identity, thereby confirming *his* true identity, that of a treacherous ruler who ruthlessly murdered me and, in doing so, irreparably broke the heart of his lovestruck daughter. The weight of the guilt, the curse—it was too much for Master Randolph. He ultimately chose to abandon any hopes for his troubled, cursed existence in favor of the possibilities his next life might bring.

Soon, any minute now, I'll be there as well, once again seeking him, *hunting* him, tracking his every move, thwarting his every plan, killing his every chance at happiness, the chance he so callously denied me."

Brow bent with intention, the old man's face suddenly softened, his eyes locating the mesmerized detective. "I pray you will grant me one final request, my good sir."

The proposition broke the trance of the spellbound detective.

The storyteller nodded at the empty mug on the adjacent table. "Would you be so kind as to fetch me some water? My looming death need not be from thirst."

The detective complied mechanically, approaching his apparently delusional subject and reaching over him for the empty glass on the adjacent table. As he did, the old man coughed violently, the convulsion pushing his frail body up against the momentarily surprised detective.

"I beg your pardon, my good sir."

The detective nodded in acknowledgement and headed toward the porcelain water jug on a small server on the other side of the room. Halfway there, upon hearing familiar words, he stopped in his tracks.

Be that word our sign of parting, bird or fiend!' I shrieked, upstarting—
'Get thee back into the tempest and the Night's Plutonian shore!
Leave no black plume as a token of that lie thy soul hath spoken!

Leave my loneliness unbroken!—quit the bust above my door!
Take thy beak from out my heart, and take thy form from off my door!'
Quoth the Raven 'Nevermore.'

Recognizing the poem, another one of his dad's favorites, the detective closed his eyes and smiled. *Edgar Allan Poe. The Raven.* Opening them, he turned his head to acknowledge the dying man's final verses, but instead his eyes caught the mirror at an angle that reflected the man reciting them from his tattered perch.

And the Raven, never flitting, still is sitting, still is sitting
On the pallid bust of Pallas just above my chamber door...

The man in the mirror, sitting upright on the bed, was anything but old. Young and vibrant, adorned in what appeared to be a linen tunic, his intense eyes cut back at the stunned detective as he dramatically delivered his poetic verses.

And his eyes have all the seeming of a demon's that is dreaming,
And the lamp-light o'er him streaming throws his shadow on the floor...

Suddenly, the man in the mirror rose to his feet. The blood drained from the officer's face realizing that, in his right hand, the young man bore a revolver, pointed at him.

And my soul from out that shadow that lies floating on the floor
Shall be lifted—nevermore!

As he spun to face the armed stranger, frantically clawing his hip side holster for the Colt revolver no longer there, the glass dropped from the detective's hand and shattered upon the hardwood floor. For a split second, his bulging eyes glanced down to confirm his missing firearm before rebounding to take in the frail old man struggling to stand while pointing the gun at him.

"My gun..." uttered the baffled officer.

"My sincerest apologies, my dear sir," offered the contrite elder. "You don't deserve this, any of it, and if I could somehow forge a different outcome, I would. You ask me why... why would a dead man steal your gun, especially since I wish you no harm and that I'll likely be dead in minutes without it? Yes, my good sir, I'll also submit that it makes no sense at all."

The armed storyteller glanced at the mirror to momentarily scan his own reflection. He sighed. "But perhaps it does. Perhaps it makes *perfect* sense. After all, wasn't I the one who triggered the death of Master Randolph by the same means, a gunshot to the head? And the more I shared with you, *confessed* to you, the more I realized that perhaps it is wholly apropos, even *poetic*, that I bring my own story full circle and—"

Mid-sentence, he fell silent, distracted by the detective's downward stare. Mouth open, the old man's bloodshot eyes followed the officer's gaze down to the expanding pool of urine surrounding his own feet.

Despite the threat posed by his own weapon, the detective briefly shared the senior's apparent embarrassment. But given his life hung in the balance, the veteran officer quickly resorted to the hostage negotiation tactics he'd learned years earlier.

Keep him talking.

"You are dying... Why on earth would you want to shoot *me*?"

A knowing smile consumed the storyteller's face. A single tear escaped his left eye.

"I would never commit such an act against one who has treated me so respectfully, my dear sir. For you have allowed me to tell my full story, one as old as time, as tragic as a Shakespearean drama. And through it all, you sat there considerately, willingly, patiently listening to my every word, my every emotion, my every poetic verse. In a hundred lifetimes, few have ever treated me so justly. If they had, I would not be standing here before you today bearing my soul in such a wretched state."

With a look of remorse, the storyteller lowered the gun. This time, his eyes and words were aimed directly at the mirror.

"What I failed to realize when I cursed the king that ancient and fateful day was that, in doing so, I cursed myself for an eternity."

The detective's body tensed and his face flashed with recognition. Instinctively, he reached for the old man.

"*WAIT!!!*"

The storyteller quickly raised the weapon to his own head, for he had a story to complete.

"And therein lies the *poetry* of it all."

The bullet exploded into the old man's skull, exiting and making a beeline to the pristine antique mirror. The detective recoiled, dropped to one knee, and covered his head with his arms as the looking glass exploded into a shower of jagged silver.

Moments later, all was silent. The detective lowered his arms and peered at the lifeless body of the storyteller, gun still in his hand.

He then glanced upon the mirror and watched spellbound as the mysterious instrument corrected itself, the bloody fissure disappearing into a liquid vortex, beginning anew.

*I*n the May 11, 1901 edition of *The Weekly Messenger*—a quarter century after the mysterious death of this book's subject—a curious article entitled "A Striking Statement" appeared in this four-page Louisiana journal published by two prominent landowners for the bayou-based communities of St. Martin Parish.

One week later, a mostly identical piece with the heading "A Bay of Oil" popped up in *The Lafayette Gazette,* a neighboring weekly published by Homer J. Mouton, an avowed white suprem-acist, son of a former lieutenant governor, and a descendant of Lafayette's founding family.

Both articles were compelling not only for their mention of a late and largely forgotten Black mystic who had spent several years in the area three decades prior, but also for their failure to acknowledge the Reconstruction-based organizing that cast him an "outside agitator" in the hostile, postbellum South. Instead, they presented a type of mystical treasure hunt, recounting in prophetic and exact terms the words of this Negro soothsayer who, upon penning a book on the afterlife during his mid-1860s stint in the region, had intuited the existence of a *"mighty bay of oil now underlying the parish of St. Martin's, La. ",* one that *"branches off to Rapides, Vermillion, Lafayette, and Calcasieu"*, a pool *"large and deep enough to furnish fuel to the world for a century."*

No small claim. At the time, the American oil industry was in its infancy, still less than a decade removed from Edwin Drake's pioneering 1859 drill at Titusville, Pennsylvania. The first oil well in Louisiana would not be drilled until June 1901 within this predicted region, 26 years after the death of the prescient Paschal Beverly Randolph.

THE GAZETTE.

PUBLISHED BY HOMER MOUTON.

Official Journal of the Town and Parish of Lafayette.

Entered at the Lafayette La. Post-Office as Second Class Matter.

SATURDAY, May 18, 1901.

A BAY OF OIL

Underlying St. Martin and Branching Off to Lafayette, Rapides, Vermilion and Calcasieu.

Nearly forty years ago a man named Paschal Beverly Randolph wrote a book entitled "After Death: The Disembodiment of Man." The book was copyrighted and published in Boston in 1868 and in 1870 a third edition was issued. Judging from the fact that Mr. Randolph's book was published three times during the first decade of its existence it is safe to say that it enjoyed a large measure of popularity. However, little or nothing was heard of the book in this section until the oil excitement caused people to search everywhere for anything which seemed to offer any light on the subject uppermost in the public mind. Mr. Randolph's opinion, expressed in 1866, will be very interesting at this time when the discovery of oil in Calcasieu and St. Martin establishes the fact that that opinion was based upon scientific observations made long before the existence of oil in these parts was even thought of. The following excerpts are from Mr. Randolph's book:

"I am, at this writing of the first edition of this book, here in the carpenter shop of Auguste Landry, in St. Martinville, St. Martin Parish, Louisiana, May 12th, 1866, over 40 years of age. Twenty-five of those years have mainly been spent in the one single pursuit of knowledge on the subject whereof I am now writing, concerning Psychical Man. I have sought for this knowledge in twelve States of this Union; in France, Ireland, Scotland, England, Turkey, Egypt, Syria, Central and Western America, Arabia, Mexico, and California."

* * * * * *

Pulled from his 1868 tome on immortality, *After Death: The Disembodiment of Man*, Randolph's extraordinary forecast did more than just detail the scope and reach of this massive body of oil as it outlined the natural geologic and carbon-based processes responsible for it being there in the first place. Mouton's *Lafayette Gazette*—along with the *Weekly Messenger* and the *Abbeville Meridional*, who described Randolph as a "sage, philosopher, seer and clairvogant (clairvoyant)"—reprinted Randolph's lengthy prediction and continued to directly reference it and him among their primary guides for oil exploration in the region.

> *Substance is but one phase of universal spirit. We see a lump of granite, and know that time and attrition will wear it down to sand; sand will divide up until we have alluvial soil, out of which comes vegetation, in various degrees of refinement, from the coarse cryptogamia to the most splendid flower and delicious fruit. Were it possible to behold the procession of the Flora pass before us in one glorious panorama, we would behold gigantic ferns and grasses, flourishing in miraculous fertility for ages; heavy carbonaceous plants, chemical laboratories of the first order, —extracting the grosser substances from the air and elaborating oxygen to fill their places. Presently —ages having elapsed —they fall and rot, making new soil and richer, out of which comes a higher order of plants, — chemical laboratories of the second order, — producing still more marked changes in the atmosphere and climate. Presently, as the picture unfolds, we behold orders, genera, and species succeeding each other at every tick of eternity's clock; finer, fairer trees and flowers now deck the scene, and animal life comes in — as chemical laboratories of a still higher order. For if vegetation alone were adequate to the preparation of the earth, air, and waters for the abode of incarnate mind, there would have been no need of animals, and there being no demand, there would have been no supply. But vegetation*

*could not do it; nor could a single species of animal do it,
but it required millions of species of differently organized
animals to prepare the world for man; to cook the air and
cleanse it; to purify the waters, and render them fit for
higher uses, just as it required a million varied flora to
throw down the noxious vapors, condense them into fibre,
to be converted by and by into coal-beds and petroleum
lakes, — just like the mighty bay of oil now underlying
the parish of St. Martin's, La., and which branches off to
Rapides, Vermillion, Lafayette, and Calcasieu, — a body
large and deep enough to furnish fuel to the world for a
century.*

—Paschal Beverly Randolph,
After Death: The Disembodiment of Man,
Randolph Publishing Company, Toledo, OH, 1868, p. 42-43.

Fourteen years after the appearance of the initial articles—and more than a decade after Mouton's untimely death—an ad in the May 22, 1915 edition of *The Weekly Messenger* continued to make this direct connection between Randolph's prediction and the prospecting it guided in the region. Entitled "Proved Oil Territory For Development," the piece opened by labeling Randolph as a "seer" before referencing his prediction and detailing how relevant interests from the well-established Martin family were relying upon it: "Imbued with this faith, we took an active interest prospecting for oil and 'Bayou Boullion' field produced at 320 feet." The ad goes on to acknowledge the Martin family's recent and inspired acquisition of close to 10,000 acres of land tracts for development in the area depicted by Randolph's mid-19th century prophecy.

By 1925, business interests in St. Martin Parish associated with *The Weekly Messenger* had launched St. Martin Oil & Gas, a company still serving the industry today.

Mouton's nearby town of Lafayette would later become known as the oil and gas capital of Louisiana and, in a March 8, 1981 article in *The New York Times,* was declared the "home of a thousand millionaires" and the "headquarters for the independent, self-made explorers and producers who are cashing in on this state's considerable piece of the greatest drilling boom of all time."

A year later, on May 26, 1982, the *New York Times* reported on the discovery of a "deep gas condensate reservoir in North Maurice Field in Lafayette Parish." At the time, the find was characterized as the "deepest productive zone" ever encountered in the field, a discovery produced under a lease and drilling agreement bearing the name of Homer Mouton.

To this day, Randolph's prophesized region continues to supply oil to the world more than a century after its discovery.

Randolph was every bit as mystical and extraordinary as his stunning prediction. Perhaps this is why history has largely chosen to ignore him. Undoubtedly, today—200 years after his birth—he is a poor fit into contemporary, sanitized accounts of our collective American past and associated efforts to bury the substantial impact of metaphysical tendencies and beliefs in the lives of our nation's most prominent historical figures be they Washington, Lincoln, or countless others.

Race has undoubtedly played a role as well, given our common conditioning that the lives of people of color born in the first half of the 19th century were either consumed by bondage or their proximity to it, and certainly not by globetrotting, intellectual pursuit, publishing, self-improvement, and metaphysical inquiry into the nature of physics, sex, the universe and God itself. If not for the massive 1996 tome, *Paschal Beverly Randolph: A Nineteenth-Century Black American Spiritualist, Rosicrucian, and Sex Magician,* by historian John Patrick Deveney—and a number of other scholars and students of Randolph's teachings—his enigmatic life may very well have been relegated to the slush pile of American history.

It should be said that truth can not only be stranger than fiction, but more magical. Despite incorporating fictitious elements, this work has traced many of the extraordinary experiences and contributions of Randolph, pulling from relevant biographies and documents as well as from his own books, speeches, and words. It is a mere, creative step in the process of ensuring that Paschal Beverly Randolph's strange truth be told for generations to come.

-D. Amari Jackson

August 2025

APPENDICES

Appendix A Randolph Updated Passport Oath
New York State, December 1861

Appendix B New York Herald Headline, Southern
Loyalists' Convention held in Philadelphia,
September 4, 1866

Appendix C Select List of Works by Randolph

Appendix D Preface of *Dealings with the Dead*, originally
published in 1861 by Randolph Publishing
(Preface by "G. D. S.")

Appendix E "A Sad Case, a Great Wrong"; Reproduction
of 1866 pamphlet with personal and
professional endorsements from President
Andrew Johnson, General Ulysses S. Grant,
Congressman Thaddeus Stevens, and other
noted statesmen

Appendix F Photo of Randolph taken by Rodney Poole
Nashville 1874

APPENDIX A

RANDOLPH UPDATED PASSPORT OATH
NEW YORK STATE, DECEMBER 1861

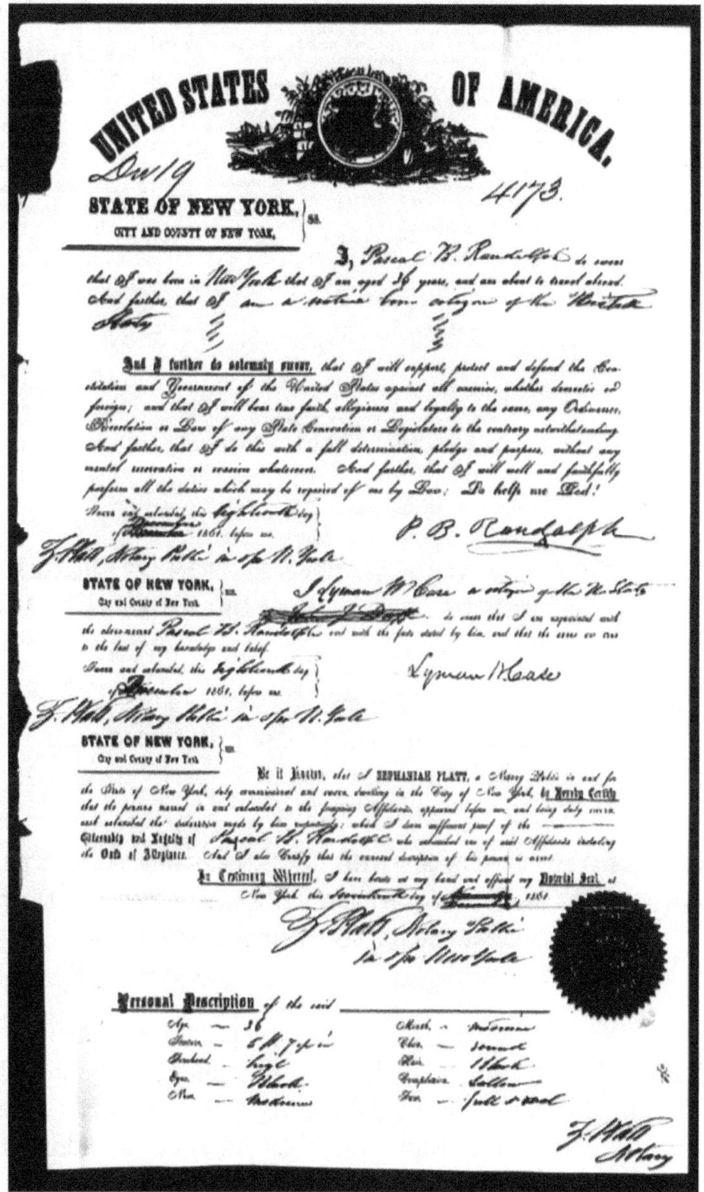

APPENDIX B

NEW YORK HERALD, TUESDAY, SEPTEMBER 4, 1866.—TRIPLE SHEET.

...a of Sinopo, Revel, New Fisher, Charleston, and Russia and America... the banquet the health States was toasted before... before paid by Russians were out in thousands, ...ox and the peasant pre-... f the Emperor appeared ...d" with enthusiasm. ...and the seat of war in ...y. The situation is one ...allies are still encamped ...ach of the Paraguayan ...t pleasure. The camp ...es are obtained, and an ...000 among those owned ...us, in the meantime, had ...on to play upon the al-...ween Chile and Uruguay, of Spanish prizes in ...celled. A strong effort ..., a plot of eighty acres ...xemption from taxation

The Nigger-Worshippers' Convention at Philadelphia.

The Convention of all the odds and ends of humanity, from the cadaverous, pale faced and canting New England parson to the blackest and strongest smelling African, met in Philadelphia yesterday. The shades of color among the conventionists were as various as the physiognomy and idiosyncrasies were remarkable. Such an aggregation of the freaks of nature, physically and mentally, in the shape of humanity, was never seen before. Our correspondents have given us graphic pen and ink sketches of some of the delegates and scenes, but it is to be hoped that one of our best photographers will not lose the opportunity of taking a picture of the motley and extraordinary assembly.

In the call for this Convention it was designated "The Southern Loyalists' Convention," but it is now called the "Loyalists' Conven-

...where on this journey that we are on the verge of a great political revolution. The people are awake; they comprehend the battle before them, and in the coming fall elections they will give the victory to the administration. This is the meaning of the President's receptions at every point along his journey.

The New Pilgrims' Progress—Brother Beecher and Ben Butler Part Company.

For a long while past Brother Beecher and Ben Butler have been travelling the same road. Butler joined Beecher at the beginning of the late war, and they both talked negro and walked along together. During the war it was interesting to observe the different deportments of the two pilgrims. Beecher, who had thrown away his Sharp's rifle, of Kansas fame, passed along with his hands folded, his lips moving in prayer and his eyes turned devoutly upward. Of course he made many stumbles, but still he

DISUNION.

First Grand National Convention of Nigger Worshippers in Philadelphia.

Renegade Southerners on the Rampage.

Blacks and Whites, Free Lovers, Spiritualists, Fourierites, Women's Rights Men, Negro Equality Men and Miscegens in Convocation.

New York Herald Headline [September 4, 1866]

DISUNION.

FIRST GRAND NATIONAL CONVENTION OF NIGGER WORSHIPPERS IN PHILADELPHIA.

RENEGADE SOUTHERNERS ON THE RAMPAGE.

BLACKS AND WHITES, FREE LOVERS, SPIRITUALISTS, FOURIERITES, WOMAN'S RIGHTS MEN, NEGRO EQUALITY MEN AND MISCEGENS IN CONVOCATION.

*The Southern Loyalists' Convention, held in Philadelphia on the first week of September 1866, was organized by individuals who remained loyal to the Union during the Civil War. Frederick Douglass attended and Randolph was allowed to address the Convention on its final day.

APPENDIX C

Select List of Works by Paschal Beverly Randolph

- 1854 *Waa-gu-Mah* (alternately *Waa-gu-Nah*)

- 1859 *Lara*

- 1859-1860 *Dhoula Bel* (aka *The Magic Globe*)

- 1860 *The Grand Secret*

- 1860 *The Unveiling*

- 1861 *It Isn't All Right*

- 1861 *Dealings with the Dead*

- 1861 *Hashish: Its Uses And Abuses*

- 1861 *Hesperina*

- 1861 *Human Love* and *Dealing with the Dead*

- 1863 *Pre-Adamite Man* (under the pseudonym "Griffin Lee")

- 1863 *The Wonderful Story of Ravalette*

- 1863 *The Celebrated "Rodney" Dream Book*

- 1863 *The Rosicrucian: His Adventures, Earthly and Unearthly*

- 1863 *The Rosicrucians—Who and What They Are*

- 1863 *Tom Clark and his Wife, their double dreams, and the curious things that befell them therein; being The Rosicrucian's Story*

- 1864 *Edward Price*

- 1866 *A Sad Case; A Great Wrong!*

- 1866 *After death; or, Disembodied man*, 1st edition

- 1867 *Clairvoyance, How to Produce It, Guide to Clairvoyance*

- 1868 *After death; or, Disembodied man*, 2nd edition

- 1869 *The Davenport Brothers*

- 1869 *Rosicrucian: Out of the Shell*

- 1869 *Love and Its Hidden History* (under the pseudonym "Count de St. Leon")

- 1870 *Seership! The Magnetic Mirror*

- 1870 *Love and the Master Passion*

- 1870 *Affectional Alchemy and How It Works*

- 1870 *The Riddle of Hermes*

- 1871 *The Asiatic Mystery*

- 1872 *James Fisk Jr. His Secret!*

- 1872 *Casca Llanna* (published anonymously)

- 1872 *The Evils of the Tobacco Habit*

- 1872 *Soul! The Soul World*

- 1872 *Will, Candy And Sugar*

- 1872 *P. B. Randolph, the Learned Pundit and Man With Two Souls, His Curious Life, Works And Career*

- 1873 *The New Mola! The Secret of Mediumship*

- 1873 *The Ansairetic Mystery*

- 1874 *Love, Woman, and Marriage*

- 1874 *The Mysteries of Eulis*

- 1874 *Eulis!: The History of Love*

- 1874 *The Ghostly Land*

- 1875 *The Book of the Triplicate Order*

- 1878 *Beyond the Veil: Posthumous Work of Paschal Beverly Randolph* (published posthumously)

- 1878 *Rosicrucian and Ashburton Springs* (published posthumously)

- 1931 *Magia Sexualis: Sexual Practices for Magical Power* (published posthumously)

APPENDIX D

Some men are daily dying; some die ere they have learned how to live; and some find their truest account in revealing the mysteries of both life and death—even while they themselves perish in the act of revelation, as is most wonderfully done in the remarkable volume now before the reader—as, alas! almost seems to be the case with the penman of what herein follows.

The criterion of the value of a man or woman is the kind and amount of good they do or have done. The standard whereby to judge a thinker consists in the mental treasures which during life they heap up for the use and benefit of the age that is, and those which are to be, when the fitful fever of their own sorrowful lives shall be ended, and they have passed away to begin in stern reality their dealings with the dead. He or she who adds even one new thought to the age becomes that age's great benefactor, to whom in future times grateful men shall erect monuments and statues. Well, here follows the work of a man, for his hand penned every line, and the ideas were born of his soul, notwithstanding his own disclaimer, for not every one can understand the mystical Blending by means of which he claims to have reached the ultima thule of human knowledge, and most readers, while reveling in the delights whereof so rich a store is laid before them, will insist that these glories were begotten of his own soul. Be that as it may, however, here is one, who, measured by the standard of the world itself, merits a monument stronger than iron, more endurable than granite, the gratitude of every soul that sighs for immortality; for not a single new thought, but whole platoons of them, grand and magnificent, hath he here presented, a deathless legacy to the world; and bye-and-bye these thoughts of 'Cynthia,' these 'Dealings with the Dead,' will become a beacon on the Highway of Thought, and be remembered to the everlasting glory of the sufferer who penned them. Rest, Paschal, rest, my brother; thou brother and lover of thy race, for thy work is well done; thy thoughts can never die. The bad will hate, but all who love Truth, Goodness, and Beauty, will bless thee, and crown thy name with fadeless laurels.

-G. D. S.

from the Preface of *Dealings with the Dead*
(originally published in 1861 by Randolph Publishing)

APPENDIX E

A Sad Case; A Great Wrong!

AND

HOW IT MAY BE REMEDIED

BEING

AN APPEAL

IN BEHALF OF

Education for the Freedmen of Louisiana.

———————

WASHINGTON, D. C.:
CHRONICLE PRINT, 456 NINTH STREET.
1866.

To the Friends of Education of all Parties, Sects, and Creeds of the United States.

In 1865 there were over a hundred schools for colored children in Louisiana. These schools were splendid in their results. They were supported by loans from the Government, to be repaid from the proceeds of a tax levied by General Banks. After the death of President Lincoln, the Board of Education was abolished, and presently the tax was suspended, school-houses returned to their owners " on taking the oath;" thousands of pupils were cast loose ; scores of teachers left in despair; dozens of schools were broken up; and, after two years of hard labor as teacher and school agent, Mr. Randolph resigned his post, and determined to seek aid from the North to enable him to establish at least *one* school not owned by persons inimical to progress and negro education. He proposes to collect means to build a house on its own land, capable of accommodating twelve hundred pupils, wherein colored aspirants to learning may be taught at the least possible money cost. Three of the departments of the proposed school we intend to be normal, that is, for the education of colored men and women for teachers. Herewith is presented, in a brief space and in a condensed form, all that is deemed essential to a correct understanding of the situation ; what the colored people of Louisiana need, and the authority upon which this appeal to the public is made.

In this place I desire to return thanks to the President of the United States for the kindness of my reception, as also to members of his Cabinet, Senators, members of Congress, and especially to Mr. Horace H. Day, by whose bounty I am enabled to print this pamphlet. But one could scarce expect different conduct from him, who has for years been foremost in many a good work. To Messrs. Sullivan and Billings, of New Orleans, to Judge Durell, Colonel Thorpe, and others, my thanks are hereby rendered for their encouragement and counsel in the great work I have undertaken.

Respectfully,

P. B. RANDOLPH, M. D.,

Special Agent Louisiana High-grade School.

WASHINGTON, August, 1866.

Many persons, wholly unfamiliar with the circumstances, blame General Baird, the Assistant Commissioner of Louisiana, for the breaking up and ruin of our schools. This is unjust, for he had no power to keep them up without funds. I think he made an error of judgment in imposing a five per cent. tax on the earnings of such freedmen as contracted with planters under the bureau, instead of imposing a capitation tax of $2 on the adult population. His plan was a failure, but he undoubtedly did the best he could. Brevet Major Studer, the present Superintendent of Education for Louisiana, is a true man, with the interest of freed people at heart. He does the best he can, but that is not much; still we hope for better things; and when the good time gets here there can be no doubt but that General Baird and Major Studer will be found on the right side, and doing their utmost toward advancing education among us. Till then, let us labor and grow strong; wait and learn wisdom; suffer, if need be, but rely wholly upon God.

Resolutions passed at a mass meeting in Thibodeauxville, on the Bayou La Fourche, concerning the proposed—

LOUISIANA HIGH-GRADE SCHOOL.

Whereas, God helps those who help themselves, and

Whereas, The road to elevation lies STRAIGHT THROUGH THE SCHOOL ROOM DOOR—and without education we are powerless—and the time has come in which it behooves us to demonstrate our manhood, and do something toward our elevation in society, and

Whereas, The Government no longer affords us educational advantages commensurate with our actual necessities, but throws us on our own resources; and

Whereas, We, the colored people of this State and parish, greatly need an educational institution, which we will support when established, and being too poor to purchase the necessary land, house, books, furniture, and apparatus; therefore,

Be it resolved, That we elect a Board of Commissioners, whose duty it shall be to take proper steps to establish such a school in our midst as we need, and that said commission be, and hereby is, composed of the following persons: Rev. James Reese, President, Oscar Crozier; Henry Enoch; Rev. William Murrill; Henry Bazile; John Burus; and are hereby duly and fully empowered to act in our behalf and that of the colored people generally.

Resolved, That Dr P. B. Randolph, our fellow-citizen of Thibodeauxville, La Fourche, Louisiana, is the proper person to direct this matter to a successful issue, by reason of his long and well-tried ability as a teacher in New Orleans, and Government school agent in this State; and that he be, and hereby is, appointed SPECIAL AGENT and Director.

Resolved, That we, through our special agent, must earnestly appeal to the Christian world; to ministers and laity of all denominations; to merchants, bankers, members of Congress, military and judicial officers, heads of departments, and to the philanthropic everywhere, to aid us in this great attempt to elevate ourselves and educate our children, and to fit us for the exercise of those high privileges which we trust one day to receive as well as deserve.

Resolved, That we, through our agent, invoke the resistless powers of the pulpit, rostrum, and press in our behalf, and humbly beg all editors of papers to forward our design.

Resolved, That as Dr. Randolph is conceded to be one of the most able and eloquent speakers on the continent, we respectfully solicit a hearing, through his lips, wherever he may go.

Resolved, That we put our trust in God, invoking his benign favor and light on our path, to the end that we may praise him *intelligently*, and educate our young men to become shining ornaments in the pulpit and society.

I certify that the above is correct, and that Dr. Randolph is duly accredited as above set forth.

JAMES REESE,

Chairman of Commission and Minister in charge of the A. M. E. Mission.

Rev. Mr. Reese is a deacon in the church, and as such, is subject to me. He is a worthy and faithful man.

JOHN TURNER,

Pastor and Elder in charge St. James' chapel, New Orleans, La.

When the schools went down Mr. Randolph immediately began to cast about for some plan whereby they might be restored, or a good large central school, with normal departments, might be established. He spoke and wrote to many persons about that matter, and subjoins a few of the many responses received:

Dr. P. B. Randolph:

If you have a plan for the establishment of a school in New Orleans, on its own ground and in its own building, I would say, carry it out by all means. I most heartily approve of the educational scheme mentioned, and sincerely hope that your efforts in the North may be crowned with success, and that you may be treated and received with due regard wherever you may go.

A. G. STUDER,

Captain and Brevet Major, and General Superintendent of Education B. R. F. and A. L., Louisiana.

The following is from Major Studer's predecessor:

HEADQUARTERS GENERAL SUPERINTENDENT OF EDUCATION, LA.

Dr. P. B. Randolph has been in the employ of this office, in the capacity of principal teacher in one of the largest and most flourishing schools for freedmen in the State. It affords me great pleasure to be able to say from an official acquaintance with him for several months past, that I have found him to be a gentlemen of very rare attainments and qualifications as a teacher, and excelled by none in sincere, earnest zeal in the great cause of education and moral elevation of the unfortunate freedmen.   I have no hesitancy in recommending him to the friends of the cause of liberty, justice, humanity, and education of the freedmen.

H. R. PEASE,

Captain, and General Superintendent of Education B. R. F. and A. L., La.

The following testimonials of character, and endorsement of the proposed school work are from some of the most illustrious men of the great Republic and the world :

Dr. P. B. Randolph, a colored man, highly recommended *as* a man; an educator of his people, a true philanthropist; and a gentleman of very rare and unusual attainments as a scholar and orator, is making a very laudable effort to establish a graded school for colored pupils, in Louisiana, wherein, in addition to juveniles, colored men and women may be instructed, and prepared to become teachers of their brethren throughout the South.

The undersigned most heartily approve thereof, and trust that he may be heard in behalf of his cause, and assisted by all who desire the advancement of civilization and refinement among the colored people of these United States.

He is EARNEST, eloquent, and true.

ANDREW JOHNSON, President of U. S.
B. F. WADE, U. S. Senator.
J. P. SULLIVAN, New Orleans, La.
T B. THORPE, New Orleans, La.
E. H. DURELL, Judge, New Orleans, La.
EDWARD C. BILLINGS, New Orleans, La.

I have known **Mr.** Randolph thirteen years and can testify to his character and qualifications, and believe him a specially qualified instrument for his work.

HORACE H. DAY, New York.

JAMES W. NYE, U. S. Senator, Nevada.

WASHINGTON, July 21, 1866.

Mr. Nye has known Mr. Randolph since 1848.

I cordially recommend Mr. Randolph and the cause he represents to the favor of the friends of the colored race, and of the country. He has energy, capacity, courage, and integrity necessary to perform the work in which he is engaged.

N. P. BANKS, M. C., Massachusetts.

WASHINGTON, D. C., July 21, 1866.

I concur in the foregoing, and commend Mr. Randolph and his cause to the consideration of the public.

WM. D. KELLEY, M. C., Pennsylvania.

I cordially sympathize with all movements similar to that of Dr. Randolph's, and believe, with proper encouragement, he will carry it forward to most desirable success.

J. B. FERGUSON,
Cor. Sec. National Union Club, Washington, D. C.

I am fully satisfied of the fitness of Mr. Randolph for the enterprise in which he is engaged, and earnestly commend him and that enterprise to public favor.

A. W. RANDALL,
U. S. Postmaster General.

I fully endorse the enterprise contemplated by Mr. Randolph.

HUGH McCULLOCH,
Secretary Treasury, U. S.

July 23, 1866.

I concur in recommending the enterprise of Mr. Randolph.

U. S. GRANT,
General, Armies of the United States.

WASHINGTON, D. C., July 24, 1866.
I heartily endorse the object proposed by Dr. Randolph, and whatever can be done, in accordance with law, I will do to aid the enterprise.

O. O HOWARD,
Major General, and Commissioner Bureau Refugee Freedmen, etc.

Dr. Randolph's character is unimpeachable; as a THINKER and author, he stands entirely alone among colored people in this country, and it is doubtful if any man of mixed blood now living is his intellectual peer. He should be encouraged in the noble work he has begun.

We heartily endorse Mr. Randolph and his enterprise. He deserves success.

THADDEUS STEVENS,
M. C. Pennsylvania.
SCHUYLER COLFAX,
Speaker U. S. House of Representatives.
E. D. McPHERSON,
Clerk House of Representatives.
JOHN W. FORNEY,
Clerk U. S. Senate.
HENRY J. RAYMOND.

Other documents to the same effect, one of which bears five hundred and eighteen signatures of colored citizens of New Orleans, many of whom are parents of children educated by Dr. Randolph, are in his possession, but are omitted here because enough has been written to set forth the situation, extent, and scope of his mission. Dr. R. has strong hopes of Congress doing something for the Schools; meanwhile the necessity of such a one as he proposes, is very great indeed, for we must and will have colored teachers, these being far less likely to be disturbed and insulted in their vocation than white ones; besides which they can always procure board which others cannot, for they can affiliate with their own people, and do as much in the cabins in the work of culture as by book and blackboard in the school-room. Moreover they will teach at far less rates of compensation, because they can live cheaper.

It has been repeatedly demonstrated that properly qualified colored teachers can advance a colored school faster in a given time than others; probably on account of the mental, physical, social, and psychical affinities which necessarily exist between them. A dozen colored teachers in New Orleans can be pointed to, whose success in teaching has indeed been wonderful. Mr. Randolph himself began with about thirteen, and ended with nearly six hundred pupils; and Chief Justice Chase, who spent an hour in one of his schools, testified his delight and surprise at the proficiency of the pupils of the " School of Progress."

Dr. Randolph proposes to give a lecture occasionally, in his own behalf, to defray personal expenses, but every dollar received for the school will be so appropriated; Messrs. Sullivan, Billings and Hughes, of New Orleans, having kindly consented to act as bankers of the funds, free of charge. G. W. Lascell, Esq., of Bennington, Vermont, will receive all contributions. All donations, therefor, may be sent to him, as, also, school material (carriage paid) that a generous people may advance for the furtherance of this great and holy cause.

Direct to " Dr. P. B. Randolph, for Louisiana High Grade School, care of G. W. Lascell, Esq., Bennington, Vermont."

MEMORIAL TABLET.

It is proposed to place a tablet on the walls of the school, bearing the names of all who shall have donated toward its establishment, as an enduring testimony of our gratitude to them, and thankfulness to our father —God.

Dr. Randolph, while in the North, will be glad to lecture in behalf of this cause whenever and wherever opportunity may afford. His address will be Bennington, Vermont, at which place letters or funds will reach him.

APPENDIX F

PASCHAL BEVERLY RANDOLPH
photo taken by Rodney Poole, Nashville 1874